BIRTH OF THE STAR DRAGON

AN EARTH FORCE SKY PATROL FILE: SOLAR YEAR 2387

BLAZE WARD

KNOTTED ROAD PRESS

Birth of the Star Dragon
An Earth Force Sky Patrol File: Solar Year 2387
Blaze Ward
Copyright © 2018 Blaze Ward
All rights reserved
Published by Knotted Road Press
www.KnottedRoadPress.com

Formerly published as *Awaken the Star Dragon*

ISBN: 978-1-64470-062-4

Cover art:

ID 11056051 © diversepixel | DepositPhoto.com

Cover and interior design copyright © 2018 Knotted Road Press

Never miss a release!
If you'd like to be notified of new releases, sign up for my newsletter.

I will never spam you, or use your email for nefarious purposes. You can also unsubscribe at any time.

http://www.blazeward.com/newsletter/

ALSO BY BLAZE WARD

The Doomsday Vault

The Last Flagship

The Hammerfield Gambit

The Hammerfield Payoff

Earth Force Sky Patrol

Birth of the Star Dragon

Flight of the Star Dragon

Call of the Star Dragon

Shadow of the Star Dragon

Trial of the Star Dragon

Other Science Fiction Stories

Myrmidons

Moonshot

Menelaus

Earthquake Gun

Moscow Gold

Fairchild

White Crane

The Collective Universe

The Shipwrecked Mermaid

Imposters

CONTENTS

PART ONE
CRIMINALS

DESPERATION

"YOU DO REALIZE that this is the stupidly, most completely-insane thing you've ever suggested, right?" his partner asked pedantically.

"So far," Morty corrected sternly, focused on the long control console in front of him. "Only so far, Xiomber. I'm sure it's going to get much worse before we're done."

"You truly believe that a *human* is the only being that can save galactic civilization from utter ruin?" Xiomber rattled on, leaning against the side of the control board but carefully not touching anything.

"Hey, a human's going to destroy everything if nobody stops him," Morty snapped. "And they even have a phrase for this, those folks: fighting fire with fire."

"Aren't two fires going to burn the house down twice as fast?" Xiomber sneered.

"We've got to find the right human," Morty replied. "The one Sarzynski is always going on about. Would you talk that way about anybody if they weren't your worst nemesis?"

"I talk about you that way all the time," Xiomber reminded him.

Morty didn't have a good response for that one. But he and Xiomber were egg-brothers, partners in science as well as in crime. And a lizard needed a friend watching his back. The galaxy was a big and dangerous place.

It had just grown bigger and more dangerous since the boss, the old boss, had decided that what he really needed was a human assassin as part of his team.

What other species could do violence without the slightest drop of empathy in them, after all? Humans weren't part of the *Accord of Souls*. Hadn't been *Uplifted* by the Elders, the grand and now long-vanished Chaa, and bound into a single, psionic whole as a way to bring peace between diverse solar tribes.

Hell, when the Chaa left, humans were still banging the rocks together, hoping someone was listening.

Who knew that they would suddenly evolve into an intelligent species and discover technology? It was all the *Accord of Souls* could do to keep humans isolated in their own home system and ignorant of everyone else. Safer that way, by far.

"You going to help or not?" Morty finally asked, looking up from the panel of knobs and gauges in front. "'Cause if not, then you need to go into the other room and not call the cops until I'm gone. That, or shoot me now, before I go and commit the worst crime imaginable on the books. Again."

He looked over at Xiomber, waiting for the damned lizard to make up his mind. Most species had a hard time reading emotions in the Yuudixtl. The Warreth probably came closest, since they had feathers that could semaphore to communicate, so they had half a clue.

Yuudixtl just had scales. Stripes and blobs and patterns that didn't really mean anything, since the Chaa had fixed their genetics when they uplifted the intelligent lizards to be one of the galactic custodians.

Xiomber was keeping his scales flat and starkly uncommunicative.

Like Morty, Xiomber was mostly kinda a gray-green somewhere a little darker than sage, but not down in that totally sexy range of a Terran crocodile. It was a shame that Yuudixtl couldn't be upgraded any further. Crocodile would be freaking awesome.

And probably useful right now, since a renegade human assassin had already killed the boss and pretty much taken over the whole organization, murdering anybody who tried to stop him or even looked at him funny.

The Yuudixtl were the smallest intelligent species in space. And maybe the smartest. They followed the basic uplift design the Chaa had selected: symmetric biped with sense organs on the head and opposable thumbs. If they were only half the height of the Vanir, and a third their mass, they made up for it in smarts.

Or had, right up until he and Xiomber had listened to Cinnra, the old Boss, and built him an illegal wormhole generator to capture a human killer, one step ahead of the human cops catching the guy, back in the Earth system.

Probably the dumbest thing they'd done, but only so far.

Morty looked forward to topping it in about five minutes.

Xiomber's dark green eyes slitted down hard and his scowl intensified.

"You're nuts," his partner repeated. "But what's the worst they could do? Throw us both in prison for two lifetimes instead of one? Scoot over."

"Me?" Marty razzed. "Why do I have to move?"

"Because you'll probably screw it up and pull the wrong guy through again."

"That was one time, and it was a chicken," Morty defended himself. "And you're the one who swore the machine was calibrated correctly."

Still, he leaned back and let Xiomber kinda hip check him out of the way. Quickly, four green hands flashed over the long rows of dials, tweaking things down and refining the target zone. They would probably only get one shot at this, because the power surge when they tripped all the generators would get someone's attention.

Maximus Sarzynski, wanna-be ultimate crime lord, would not take it well, him and his egg-brother digging up the guy's worst enemy and pulling him halfway across the galaxy as an insurance policy.

And unlike the Uplifted Species in the *Accord of Souls*, *Maximus* could kill them without the slightest hesitation or provocation. Just what old Cinnra had wanted in an hired gun.

He had only really screwed up when he thought that he could control a *human* afterwards.

"You figured out how we escape?" Xiomber asked out of the side of his mouth. "Those damned birds will roll over as soon as the new Boss yells *boo*. Then they're coming after us. And we sure as hell can't go to the cops with something like this."

"Kinda planning on cheating," Morty replied. "That's why I wanted you in the other room if you weren't going to help."

"Oh, *fardel*," Xiomber snapped. "Now what?"

"After we grab the human, I was going to redirect him right through another wormhole, and jump in after him," Morty said carefully. "This controller is kinda programmed to overload and eat itself, so nobody can chase us, or figure out where we went."

"Are you sure we came from the same egg batch?"

Xiomber growled. "'Cause I don't remember any of my siblings being that dumb. Where do you think they'll look?"

"I'm not sending him to *Yuudixtl*," Morty replied. "Like you figured, first place Maximus will look."

"Where then, Morty?" his partner got serious. Way serious. Like maybe *thinking-about-overcoming-the-empath-bond-so-he-could-kill him* serious. "Where you are dumping us out?"

"*Orgoth Vortai*," Morty said in a quiet, careful voice, expecting to get punched in the snout.

Instead, Xiomber turned and stared at him for several seconds, jaw agape. And then he started laughing.

Morty relaxed and zeroed down the last few gauges. The range was stupid long for a shot like this, doubly so on a bounce-tube, but they also had an exact match of the psionic coordinates that had located Maximus the killer in the first place. All Morty had needed to do was flip them end for end and find the man who was Sarzynski's psionic opposite.

A good guy.

"You ready to do this?" Morty asked as Xiomber settled down.

"Why the hell not?" Xiomber said. "I always wanted to visit the world of the tentacle-heads. With any luck, they'll look at the whole, damned thing as a monstrous art installation. Maybe a performance piece for the ages."

"That was actually part of my original logic," Morty admitted. "They already do crazy shit. What's one thing more?"

He reached out and grabbed the second-to-last slider, ramming it to the top of the scale with a hard click. Several floors below, a dozen generators began to hum. In moments, they were singing. Shortly, the metal would begin to scream.

Around them, overhead lights flickered and then a few exploded, throwing rooster tails of sparks and smoke in all directions as Morty's device started pumping too much power through the entire building. At least nobody would be using this tube generator station again.

But boy, was Maximus going to be pissed.

"Ready?" Morty yelled.

"Do it," Xiomber shouted over the rising din. "We're not going to hold this much longer."

Morty grabbed the last slider and pushed it slowly forward.

"Energizing," he hollered back.

In the area beyond the control console, a golden nimbus of energy formed, and quickly resolved itself into a pair of tube openings, like a hose that had been sliced neatly in half.

Morty stared hard at the zone controls, watching the screen's targeting array home in on the target he had selected.

"Almost got it," he yelled, starting to smell smoke rising.

The console was probably close to catching fire, with the energy they were processing through it.

"Now, Morty," Xiomber screamed. "It's not going to stay intact much longer."

Morty slammed a fist down on the big, purple button and listened to the generators reach for that last two percent.

Definitely getting bright in here. Maybe a little warm.

"Let's go," he scrambled around the console and began to run towards the nexus of the bounce-tube.

"What if you missed?" Xiomber was a step behind him.

"Then our goose is right cooked when Maximus finds out, and we've got nobody to hide behind," Morty replied.

Something was coming through the first tunnel. Morty could see the left-hand tube pulsate, like a snake swallowing a rat. Hope to the Gods this worked, because he also saw a door open at the far end of the lab.

"What's going on in here?"

FIELD AGENT

GARETH ST. JOHN DANKWORTH. Field Agent of the Earth Force Sky Patrol.

Gods, that sounded awesome. And looked even better. He had finally made it. He was a Field Agent now. Lawman extraordinaire. Respected across the entire Solar System.

Gareth stared again at his reflection in the wall mirror of his quarters. He was at **The Arsenal**, Sky Patrol's base in the Earth/Moon L2 point, over beyond the dark side of the moon. Affectionately called **Shadow Base One**.

His new uniform was amazing. Still the black riding boots and white hotpants of a Sky Patrol Agent, but now his maroon tunic finally said *Field Agent*. Three white rings around the big, stylized SP in the center of his chest, offset by gold buttons up both sides of the bib and the gold wing-protectors on his shoulders like short fins.

He tugged the tunic down a little, settling it a little tighter beneath the black, Sam Brown belt. He ran a hand back through his curly, blond hair, just getting long enough to blow in the wind, so it was probably time to get it shorn again, as it had reached the maximum length that the regulations allowed.

Field Agent.

Damn, he looked good.

Best of all, he could finally propose to Philippa, after they had both waited for so long, both of them staying chaste and pure, until he could make it all the way to Field Agent and they could be married. Gareth reached a hand down into his pocket and pulled out the tiny, leather pouch he kept with him at all times.

From inside, he extracted the gold ring with the single, white diamond in the middle, surrounded by ruby and gold stones representing Sky Patrol. Tonight was the night. He'd catch a shuttle over to the Earth/Moon L1 point in an hour. She was working as a research assistant for her father these days, at Earth Force Headquarters, so it would be easy enough to take her aside after dinner, during a walk along the Promenade overlooking the Moon's bright side, and propose to her properly.

He was a Field Agent now. All that waiting would be over, and they could finally become man and wife.

He smiled at the ring, tucking it back into the pouch and stashing it in his pocket.

Not long now.

A sound brought his head up.

It was a strange humming sound, almost imperceptible, hovering right at the point of audibility. Almost as if a fly was trying to sneak around the room behind him, but wasn't succeeding.

Gareth looked all directions with a concerned scowl on his face. He was in his personal quarters at The Arsenal. Nobody ever came in except the cleaning crew, so the room was as pristine as his bunk had always been in school, bed made so taut that a shilling coin could bounce a foot high.

Except that the room had taken on a golden hue. Odd.

There was nothing wrong with the lights. They still put out the perfect, crisp white of the fifth generation organic diodes, but the air itself was turning golden.

Bizarre.

And now something faded into existence across the room, like a film of fog melting, only run in reverse. This mirage appeared to be the source of the gold, and it was growing, both in size and intensity.

Panic woke up at the back of Gareth's brain. He had always been noted for his bravery and leadership, but today, those parts of his mind seemed to be having second thoughts. There was no science he could think of that explained a portable whirlpool suddenly appearing in the air in the middle of his cabin.

Maybe it was time to do something.

A wind came up suddenly, inside his cabin at the center of a space station, ruffling his hair as greedy fingers began to pluck at his soul.

His soul?

Very much not good.

Gareth sprang into action, like the hero he had always been. He raced to the door, keying the internal telephone system and picking up the headset.

"Base Operator," a woman's bored voice answered.

"This is Field Agent Dankworth," he said, voice struggling to remain calm. "Cabin 24-575. Something's happening in my room. Something bad."

"Could you be clearer, Field Agent?" the laconic operator replied. It sounded like maybe she had one hand up, inspecting her nails as she spoke.

"I've got an emergency here, miss," he yelled, feeling those golden fingers begin to caress his back.

The wind was stronger now, tugging insistently closer to the hole in the universe that was growing over in the corner.

Hole in the universe?

"Please state the nature of your emergency," she replied, maybe reading from a script now.

Gareth tried to think of the right words, but the pull of the tempest was too great now. Fight it as he tried, the force literally dragged him across the cabin, stretching the cord of the handset until it was pulled right out of his hands, falling to the wall with a thunk as Gareth's legs went numb.

Looking down, his lower half appeared to be fading out of existence, right at the event horizon of that golden light. The golden fingers crept up his nerves, pulling him under with grim determination.

Oh, shit.

WORMHOLE

IT WAS like going down a waterslide as a kid, vacationing with his parents at a theme park dedicated to the South Seas, back home in Indiana. Gareth couldn't see anything except the sides of a golden tube of light, but when he put his hand out to touch, they pulled back.

He couldn't fall any slower, or faster, regardless of what he did. And it felt like he was simultaneously the size of a mouse and of a whale.

Screaming like a little girl didn't seem to help, either. Or rather, nobody was listening, which was probably good. Gareth wondered if he was going to keep on falling forever.

There, in the distance between his toes, Gareth saw something. Darkness, perhaps. A gap. Maybe the end of the tunnel, thank God.

He seemed to be slowing down. Or something.

Yes. The tunnel ended there. He could sense a room just beyond it.

Gareth felt his brain and his soul drop back into phase with the rest of the universe. What the name of Heaven was that?

He found himself standing in a clearing. Surrounded by trees out of the worst nightmares the ancient artist Dali had ever dreamt up: bark the wrong color, trunks somehow the wrong shape, and with leaves that looked like nothing so much as feathers.

The space here was that same golden hue of his cabin, and the tunnel.

Standing in front of him were a pair of three-foot-tall lizards, dressed in pants and t-shirts, standing upright and eyeing him like dinner. Gareth would have given a month's salary to be holding his Sonic Stunner right now, but it was safely locked up, back at The Arsenal.

Wait, lizards?

The room howled as well. Gareth considered joining it, but one of the lizard-men hopped into the air and tossed something into his mouth, rather like a jelly bean.

Jelly bean? What the hell is wrong with you people?

Gareth went to spit it out, but the bean had already dissolved and melted itself to his tongue, like the best peanut butter on a PBJ sandwich.

Gareth chewed frantically, trying to escape its clutches.

"That work?" the closer lizard-man asked.

Gareth turned, utterly shocked that these things spoke English. Had somebody slipped a Mickey Finn into his drink at dinner? Was this all some sort of hallucination as part of a failed seduction attempt? Who would he wake up next to in the morning?

He chewed, unable to speak. The one who had spoken wore a logo on his shirt, but it honestly looked like an old, ratty concert T-shirt, rather than the more stylized *Sky Patrol* **SP** on Gareth's chest.

"You can understand me?" the lizard asked. "Just nod."

Gareth complied, nightmares of Alice and toadstools

haunting him. He scanned the feathered trees nearby for Cheshire Cats.

"We need to get gone," the other lizard-man told the first. "Somebody's going to remember us."

"Okay," the first said, staring hard at Gareth like he was a badly-trained puppy. "You need to come with us, so we can get someplace private and I can explain everything. This is not a dream, but it could become a nightmare, without too much effort. Are you safe to touch?"

"What?" Gareth managed around the peanut butter. "What's the meaning of this?"

The lizard-man sighed and his shoulders slumped. A twinkle came into his eyes after a second and he smiled.

"Humans are the most dangerous, lethal species in the galaxy, okay?" he said. "You've been kept confined in your solar system until you matured enough to not be a threat to everyone else, which is not today. Except one of your kind got loose, and it threatening to destroy all galactic civilization. Nobody can stop this killer, so we took a gamble and kidnapped you. You might be the only person who can save us."

Gareth felt a surge of pride rush through him. Earth Force Sky Patrol. The Good Guys.

Field Agent Gareth St. John Dankworth, ready to serve.

He stood taller, shoulders back and head up. Which kind of ruined the scene, since these two might have been three and a half feet tall.

"Who is my foe?" Gareth announced boldly. "What do I need to do?"

The two lizard-men shared a glance, and a smile, it seemed.

"Marc Sarzynski," the first one said. "Called *Maximus*."

"That bastard's here?" Gareth growled in shock. "No wonder he escaped me. Where are we?"

"The planet is named *Orgoth Vortai*," the second one said. "Home of a species known as The Grace."

"Species?" Gareth wasn't sure he heard the word right.

"You got it, pal," the first said. "There are over a dozen sentient, technological species in the *Accord of Souls*. The Grace are not quite the weirdest, but they're close. And when one wants to talk to you, and they will, be prepared to be touched. Now, can we go get some tea and hide out?"

"Maximus is here?" Gareth reiterated.

"Not on this planet, but we know where he is, once you're ready," the tiny lizardman said.

"And I'm not stoned out of my mind on Bennies and Smack?" he continued.

"On what?" the second one asked.

"Mind-altering, hallucinogenic narcotics," Gareth explained. "Humans take them as an escape from everyday life."

"Nope, we need you sober, pal," the first lizard-man said. "It's already going to be weird enough as is."

"What was that thing you put in my mouth?" Gareth asked, finally having swallowed the last bits. Or maybe they had dissolved completely.

"A transform virus programmed for humans," the little man said. "It inoculated you against most diseases, as well as programmed your brain to be able to speak our language. You don't think the rest of us spoke English, do you?"

"Oh," Gareth said. "Maybe I do need a drink."

"Tea first," the lizard-man said. "I'm sure we'll need something stronger later. Ready to join us?"

"Yeah, I think so," Gareth said, pretty unsure of all of this, but willing to stay put. Maybe.

"Good," the first said. "Now, we're going to exit this park, cross a couple of blocks, and hit a tea shop nearby. If anyone asks, you're just a runt Vanir, okay? Humans are the absolute embodiment of evil, as far as anyone knows, but nobody really knows what a human looks like, and you're close enough to pass for a Vanir for now. We good?"

"What are your names?" Gareth asked. "I am Field Agent Gareth St. John Dankworth, of the Earth Force Sky Patrol, Missile Division, 6th Cavalry Troop."

"Yeah, and if you ever mention that again, your ass will be in a jail cell so fast your head will spin, pal," the one said. "Ours right beside you. We'll never see the light of day again, and Maximus will end up Emperor of the Universe. So keep it quiet. We'll just call you Gareth, for now. I'm Morty, and this is my egg-brother, Xiomber. Let's go."

Gareth found himself following the first little lizardman. He had been so focused earlier he hadn't even really processed the fact that he was standing in a small clearing of an arboreal forest of some sort, next to a thing that looked remarkably like a bizarre garden maze, except the walls were only four feet tall and made of a weird mix of metal, wood, and flowering plants, with lots of open spaces allowing sunlight and breezes through.

He glanced up, trying to measure the time, and stopped so fast that Xiomber ran into him from behind.

"Hey, friend," Xiomber barked. "Little warning next time?"

"The sky…" Gareth's words tapered off.

It was close enough to noon, with the sun more or less overhead. But the sky was pink-orange, somewhere between cotton candy and first-run salmon from back home.

THERE WAS NO BLUE, ANYWHERE IN THE SKY!

"Quieter, please, Gareth," Morty smacked him on the thigh, breaking the hypnotic spell that had fallen over him. "You're not on Earth anymore, m'kay? This is *Orgoth Vortai*. C'mon."

Right.

Gareth fell in behind Morty again, walking in a calm daze. Alien planet named *Orgoth Vortai*. Sure. Surrounded by talking lizardmen. Why the hell not?

The trees ended suddenly and Gareth was on a sidewalk. Maybe. Whatever the local, planetary equivalent was.

And it was moving. Both of them. Wow. There was a path moving to the right, with a second one, closer to the street, moving to the left.

And people.

People? Sure, why not? I'm completely stoned now. Whatever they gave me has gone all the way in and now I'm riding the lysergic acid all the way to the end of the rainbow, where I'll find the leprechaun level monster, waiting for me to fight him to the death for his pot of gold.

Gareth must have stopped walking again. Xiomber just stepped up and took his hand, like a child leading a parent around a theme park.

They got on the moving sidewalk, and Gareth smiled politely at the woman in front of him as she turned and studied him.

Except it wasn't a woman. Or, maybe it was. She had curves. A fantastic bottom, narrow waist, ripe bosom contained in some sort of silky wrap that looked like a fairies' cocoon.

But her skin was green. And her eyes had slits, kinda like Morty and Xiomber, rather than irises. Like a snake, or a cat. Except she looked like a snake, with long, green-black hair. Except that wasn't hair. Those were snakes.

She was a medusa.

Gareth nearly screamed again, but Xiomber jerked his hand hard enough to nearly make him fall over. He rounded angrily on the little man.

"You're staring," Xiomber growled quietly up at him. "It's impolite. And she might take it as invitation to talk. Those tentacles on her head? You know, where you have hair and I have a bone crest? Those are sensors pods that combine touch, taste, and smell. The Grace are a very tactile species. Let's not today, okay?"

Tactile. Right. All those snake-hair-thingees slithering over his skin?

If he ignored the tentacles, she was an amazingly beautiful woman.

Medusa.

Something.

Maybe she'd turn him to stone, if he wasn't careful.

Or if he was lucky.

Gareth smiled weakly at her and turned his attention to the rest of the city.

Oh My God!

Earth had nothing like this. It was like a fairy tale, with impossibly tall buildings of all shapes and colors. Some were stone. Others were glass. A few appeared to be forests that had been transformed, like a giant's banzai tree experiment, plopped down in the middle of a city.

The woman behind them on the sidewalk smiled as he accidentally made eye contact.

Gareth managed not to scream. And pulled his mouth shut and held it there by grinding his teeth. She was a cat. No, a lynx, covered over with cream and gray fur, standing more than five and a half feet tall, wearing harem pants and loose top in matching baby blue silk. The face was close enough to human that it might be a mask, once he got past the magnificent, muttonchop sideburns and the ears on top, except that her ears moved, one rotating towards him like a radar dish as he watched in awe.

"Morty, we need to debark," Xiomber said loud enough that the other turned. "Now."

Xiomber tugged his hand and Gareth stumbled briefly as they landed on the sidewalk.

The lady-lynx kept riding by, but handed him a business card written in vermillion ink as she passed him with a hopeful smile. The smell on the card was almost enough to make Gareth chase after her.

"What are you?" Xiomber groused in awe. "Bottled animal magnetism? Morty, we gotta get this one undercover quick, before we've got a mob of horny women after us. That's two already."

There was a break in the traffic going the other way. The one called Morty bolted through it. Xiomber followed, dragging Gareth along numbly.

He was still holding the card, sniffing her scent. She made him feel all tingly inside, and kinda goofy. But it also let Xiomber pull him easier.

Traffic magically seemed to part around them, and Morty ducked into a shop, the other two in quick pursuit.

Now he'd gone blind.

Except, not blind. Sun blind. There. Man, it was dark in here. Okay, table. Bench. Sit. Good. Sniff card. Wow.

"Put that away," Morty snapped. "I need you coherent. Not dunk on the scent of a Nari in season."

"A what?" Gareth asked weakly.

"That woman on the slidewalk," Morty pointed back over his shoulder. "She's a Nari. She gave you a scent marker. Didn't think Nari did that, outside of their own kind. It's frightening, the power you have over women, pal. In other circumstances, we'd put that to use, but right now we need to hide."

Reluctantly, Gareth pulled out his wallet and slipped her card in with the others he had accumulated from scientists and politicians he had met. It was sized close enough to fit.

The two lizardmen were eyeing him when he looked up.

"What?" he asked, nervous.

"Nothing," Morty said.

Gareth watched him signal to a waitress. She was another of The Grace, although not as voluptuous as the first. If she were human, Gareth would have guessed her to be a teenage girl, perhaps. Petite and thin.

This one smiled, too, but Morty growled for her to get the tea if she wanted a tip, so she just winked at Gareth and sashayed away. She also had a mesmerizing bottom.

"Hey, pal," Xiomber cracked wise. "Eyes over here, please."

"Right," Gareth reluctantly turned to the others, trying to figure out why he was here. Wherever here was. "So the two of you are criminals, engaged in a major felonious enterprise, and somehow I'm both the crime and the prize?"

"A little louder next time, maybe?" Morty snapped. "I don't think the cook heard you in back. You wanna be in jail?"

"Sorry," Gareth dropped to a murmur. "A little excited here. I've never been on an alien planet before. What's next?"

"Now, we hide you from Maximus until we can get you to a lab and make some improvements to you," Morty said. "Maximus has been doing the same to himself, but I don't think he dreams big enough. At least not yet."

"Maximus," Gareth growled, remembering he was a cop. "What's he doing now? And how do we stop him?"

Gareth watched the two share a guilty glance silently for a moment. Morty shrugged.

"So until about ten minutes ago, we were members of a criminal gang," Morty began in a voice so quiet Gareth had to lean all the way down close to hear. "Our old boss, Cinnra, was a Warreth scientist, with aspirations of taking over the whole criminal underworld, across the entire *Accord of Souls*."

"What's a Warreth?" Gareth asked carefully, trying not to talk so loud that he got arrested just when the little man got to the good parts.

Xiomber leaned in and cut his brother off.

"Think birdman, Gareth," he said simply. "Earth has lots of bird species, so imagine a humanoid a little shorter than you, about half your mass, covered with feathers."

"Birdman," Gareth acknowledged. "Got it."

Sure. Why the hell not?

"So Cinnra had us build a very illegal, psionic wormhole generator, and locate him a human assassin," Morty continued. "This would have been about, uhm…"

He paused, apparently doing some math in his head, eyes fixed on some strange spot on the ceiling.

"Maybe five Earth months ago?" Morty asked. "I think."

"That was when Sarzynski escaped me," Gareth snarled quietly. "We had him holed up with his gang. He escaped, and they all swore it was some weird gold light that did it. Oh, shit. Gold light. You guys."

"Yup," Xiomber noted with pride. "Boss nailed down the shape of the psionic signature he wanted in a human, and had us program it into the scanner. Bada-bing, bada-boom, and Bob's your uncle."

"Uhm, what?"

"He said we located our target and extracted him, one step ahead of the arm of law enforcement," Morty explained. "You, given all the bitching Maximus has done about you since then."

"Oh," Gareth said with his own surge of pride. "So you recruited an assassin?"

"Yeah, but Cinnra thought he could control the human," Morty said. "Found that out the hard way when Maximus turned on him."

"What did the rest of the gang do?" Gareth asked.

"Went along with it," Morty said. "The human's a freaking killer. Our choices were pretty stark here. Your kind are not known for being the forgiving types, you know?"

"We're not all like that," Gareth replied.

He wanted to say more, but the young girl with the tentacles returned with a cast iron tea pot and three mugs. She set the pot down in the center of the table by leaning past Gareth.

He flinched and nearly screamed when several of her tentacles caressed his hair and neck.

"Hey," Morty snapped. "You want me to get the manager out here?"

"Sorry," she purred, withdrawing dreamily.

Gareth watched her face turn nearly umber with blush as she stepped back.

His subconscious couldn't decide if the feeling had been feathers caressing him, or teeth looking for a place to bite. Or both.

Xiomber poured a mug and handed it to him, before serving them. Gareth sipped carefully, but the taste was yummy.

"So that thing you put in my mouth," he asked after a moment. "How'd you know that would work? You said Maximus and I were the only humans here."

"We reprogrammed him the same way," Xiomber explained. "We can do that with humans, because they aren't part of the *Accord of Souls*."

"What do you mean: *reprogram*?" Gareth felt an uneasy tide nibble at his toes.

"The Chaa uplifted all the species to sentience a long time ago," Morty said. "Before they left, as a matter of fact, and turned most of their own kind into the Vanir. *Those Left Behind*. But they also fixed everyone's genetics pretty hard.

We can eliminate disease and all that, but nobody can be improved past where the Masters left us all."

"Except humans?" Gareth guessed. "And Maximus is upgrading himself? Like bad?"

"He's improved his brain, so he's way smarter than he used to be," Xiomber explained.

"That's bad," Gareth replied. "Marc Sarzynski was a renegade from the Sky Patrol. Part of my class of Agents, before he went bad. Turned criminal. But he was already at the top of the pack, then. If he's smarter now, you're in trouble. We're in trouble."

MAXIMUS

"YOU'RE sure what it was that you observed?" Marc Sarzynski asked again, scowling heavily at the men of his gang, arrayed below him in the space that he thought of as his throne room.

It had been Cinnra's personal aerie, once upon a time. Marc liked the vaulted ceilings above him, as well as the stone slabs stepping down from where he had put his throne. Each was about ten yards across by twenty wide, and the whole room was a series of steps. The only change he had made was to have a couple of Yuudixtl add stair steps everywhere, so all the non-gliders could get around here easily, and not just the Warreth.

He was recruiting more, these days, and going outside the insular Warreth clans that had been the basis of Cinnra's power. The gang would need to feel more comfortable in here.

Marc scanned the mob of aliens a level below him, nearly a hundred faces from strange nightmares staring back. Five months ago, he had never even imagined that aliens existed. And now he had at least twelve species actively serving him.

The Warreth male at the center flattened his headcrest some as he spoke, an unconscious reflex that Marc had finally learned was the equivalent of a dog tucking his tail under. Body language of submission. It was good, being in charge. Things would get done around here, finally.

"The generators had all started running at once, so I went into the lab to see what was going on," Deoar said, somehow pitching his voice loud while not sounding threatening.

The survivors of the takeover had all learned that lesson.

"When I got there, Xiomber and Morty had powered up the wormhole generator and were pulling someone through," the birdman continued.

The creature reminded Marc of a Stellar Jay, with blue and black feathers, even though his beak was nowhere near as long as it would have been. Deoar's was shorter, almost petite. Just enough to crack walnuts, rather than dipping into flowers.

"So somebody came through the first tube," Deoar said. "Just as I entered the room. Then they bounced him out using a second tube and jumped in right after him. About that moment, the console overloaded and I had to concentrate on putting out the fires, but I know what I saw."

"Describe it again," Marc said in a voice that couldn't help but be threatening. His nerves were shot this morning. It was not possible, what Deoar had described.

"Before I met you, boss, I would have said a short Vanir," the birdman continued. "But I'm pretty sure it was a human. Same build, but not as tall. About what you used to be, a little taller than me. Golden hair."

"Yes, yes," Marc said. "The clothing. What was he wearing."

"Garnet jacket with gold letters on a black logo and gold shoulder pieces," Deoar replied. "Three white rings around the logo on the chest. White pants. Black boots."

"And golden hair?" Marc confirmed.

"You got it, boss."

Marc slammed one first down onto the armrest of the new throne but otherwise contained his emotions. Fear was a useful thing, in small doses. It would not do to completely frighten his people out of their wits.

"Ladies and gentleman, I should be possessed of an anger for the very gods, right now," he pronounced, watching the five score aliens below him recoil half a step at the thought, anyway. Yes, fear of god was a thing they understood. "And I will exercise that rage on those two little traitors when we find them. Xiomber and Morty are to be killed, without mercy. But today is also our lucky day. They've managed to locate my worst enemy and actually bring to me, here in the *Accord of Souls*. The human Deoar has described is a Field Agent of the Earth Force Sky Patrol. For humans, the equivalent of the Vanir Constabulary, with just about as much sense of humor. That human is most likely Gareth St. John Dankworth."

Marc rose from his throne and began to pace. He had the entire top platform to himself. Skylights overhead cast him in alternate spotlights and shadows as he moved.

"They will probably not have taken him to Yuudixtl, but alert our agents there anyway," Marc commanded. "Instead, we need to be on the lookout for another human loose in *Accord* space. Perhaps we should alert the authorities, as well."

Marc picked out a Nari male off to one side. Unlike most of the gang, Zorge was older, well into Nari middle-age, with white fur coming in along the edges of the orange and gray stripes. And he had actively chosen a life of crime, rather than being forced into it by circumstances.

If the cat-man had possessed any greater ambitions in life, Marc probably would have had to kill him when he first took over, but Zorge was content working as a spy, maneuvering in the shadows. All he wanted to do was run his own little network of informants. It was good.

"Pass an anonymous tip to the Vanir," Marc ordered the old cat. "Let them know that there is a *human* loose in Accord space. Emphasize the golden hair, though."

That got a laugh as Marc ran a hand back through his own pitch-black curls. In that, he looked much more like a typical Vanir, darker of skin and hair than Dankworth. And a foot taller, these days. If the so-called, self-appointed, Custodians of Order weren't so damned tall, a human like Gareth could have easily passed himself off as one, but the women alone were six and a half feet tall, and the men usually seven. Freaking giants.

Like Maximus was now.

Morty and Xiomber had been in the process of researching how to rebuild him again, even better than the Vanir he appeared to be. He already had the perfect disguise, so perhaps their betrayal now was in his best interests. Internally, Marc shuddered at the thought of what those two damnable, lizard scientists might have done to him, had he put himself under their care for greater transformation when they were intent on duplicity.

The room had fallen silent at his introspective pacing. They knew better than to interrupt, but no new genius insight bubbled up right now. He was still getting used to having an IQ of two hundred by human standards.

"Find him," Marc growled to his mob. "Bring him to me."

TEA ROOM

GARETH HAD SETTLED DOWN SOME. The tea was amazingly good in this place, a gentle blend of vanilla, caramel, oolong, and some sort of berry that just seemed to fill in all the happy spaces in his soul.

Briefly, he wondered if the twins had added something to the jelly bean they had fed him, to make him calmer than he should have been. Probably not the worst idea, given their opinion of humans.

Morty was off, making a phone call to someone. And possibly having a smoke, if Gareth understood the vernacular correctly. He would need to have a chat with the Yuudixtl scientist later on the evils of tobacco, or whatever it was.

Xiomber had run to the men's room, leaving Gareth alone for the briefest moment.

Keelee had just delivered a second pot of tea, leaning so close that she briefly seemed to press one breast against his shoulder in ways that made Gareth extremely self-conscious. Worse, at least half a dozen tentacles had taken their time tasting him.

Or whatever The Grace called it. It was positively

pornographic, the way her tentacles caressed his skin, ran through his hair, idled at the edge of his collar. She seemed to hum, or perhaps purr, as she did so.

Gareth realized he was never, ever going to ogle a waitress in a public house again. Or perhaps any woman. His own behavior had never been all that bad, but suddenly he was on the receiving end of what his men had frequently done to those poor women they had encountered at landfalls, trapped by the need to remain quiet in a bar, rather than staging a loud, emotional scene in public that would get them fired. If Gareth reacted loudly, called attention to the treatment he was receiving, he'd be arrested.

By the Gods, he would be much more of stickler for the rules, if he ever got home. This sort of thing was just embarrassingly rude.

As was the way he seemed to be enjoying the feel of Keelee's tentacles exploring his skin.

Thoughts of Philippa suddenly flashed to mind and he sat bolt upright.

"Keelee, you need to stop now," he demanded weakly. "Xiomber will be back soon, and I don't want you to get fired."

She laughed, throatily, but withdrew, the most polite sandpaper to ever set his nerves afire. Gareth breathed heavily and concentrated on pouring himself more tea.

Burning his throat seemed like a good idea right now, but he blew on the mug anyway.

Morty and Xiomber returned at the same moment from different directions.

"*Fardel*," Morty swore quietly. "You left him alone?"

"I wasn't sure if you were coming back, Morty," Xiomber snapped. "And I really had to pee. Besides, it's not like he was going anywhere."

"You okay, kid?" Morty asked Gareth. "You look a little flustered."

"Huh?" Gareth looked over at the tiny man. "What?"

"I know a guy," Morty said. "Had to skip my usual contact here, because she's a she and I don't need that level of complication right now. Let's go. We need to get you changed into something a lot less obvious, and then off this planet before any of the old gang tracks us down."

"You find us a lab?" Xiomber asked.

Gareth watched the other twin pull something from his back pocket and hold it up. It was almost a floppy wallet, but it was as big as his palm and barely half an inch thick. Looked like leather, though.

"Remember, I got everything here we need, but we still need to baseline the monkey-boy before we get crazy," Xiomber continued.

"That's next," Morty said, digging into a pocket and pulling out several coins that he dropped on the table.

"Did you leave a tip for Keelee?" Gareth asked.

"Who?"

"Our waitress," Gareth replied.

"How did you know…crap, she tasted you, didn't she?" Morty snarled.

"It wasn't that bad," Gareth protested defensively.

"Except now she can describe you to the cops," Morty hissed angrily. "We gotta get gone, right now."

Gareth followed them out into the street. Morty pulled out a pocketcomm similar to the one Gareth would have had with him, except it was sitting on his dresser, back at The Arsenal, along with his money, his ID, and his Sonic Stunner travel vault.

Morty pressed a button and looked up. Within moments, a flying car dropped out of the sky like a gray hawk, landed right in front of them, and a side door full-winged open.

"Get in," Morty commanded.

Gareth more or less fell into the vehicle, finding the back of the sky chariot a comfortable cocoon of crushed blue velvet. He sat on the bench facing forward, with Xiomber next to him and Morty across the way. The seat belts were more or less intuitive, but the two Yuudixtl didn't move to put theirs on.

"Seatbelts?" Gareth prompted.

"Seriously?" Xiomber glanced up, but he huffed and pulled the straps on. A moment later, Morty did the same. "Morty, we gotta talk about this guy."

"Dead or Jail, Xiomber," Morty reminded his brother. "Those are your other choices."

Gareth discovered that a Yuudixtl could roll his eyes, just like a human. With the same level of apparent teen angst and *ennui*.

Some things were apparently universal.

The car leapt into the air, driving Gareth back into the seat and reminding him why the seatbelts were such a good idea. A moment later, the car banked hard and shot off horizontally. Gareth probably would have ended up on top of Xiomber if he hadn't been already strapped down.

Xiomber looked up and came to the same conclusion. The grumbling under his breath ceased.

Outside, an exotic wonderland of a magical city swept by. Towers and sky bridges and flying cars.

And an angel.

Gareth found himself with his nose pressed against the glass of the window and his hands up, like a six-year-old on a long drive.

Maybe an angel. Human-looking, with wings that looked

twenty feet wide as it flapped, holding a pocketcomm in his hands and watching something.

"Wazzat?" he almost drooled on the glass.

Morty leaned over and peeked.

"Elohynn," he said. "One of the *Accord* Species. Empaths. Damned good counselors. Right bastards as bankers, though.

"How many species are there?" Gareth asked, watching the man fade into the distance as the taxi sped away and then slipped around a corner.

"Seventeen," Xiomber asked. "Three others are candidates, in another few thousand years. Humans are not, however. Too freaking dangerous."

"You keep saying that," Gareth turned to the scientist. "Why?"

"The *Accord of Souls* didn't have a word for murder, Gareth," he replied flatly. "We had to use yours. Same goes for all the different levels of killing you crazy barbarians to do each other. Some people might pass out, just hearing the word *xenocide*. If the Chaa were still around, they might have either fixed you, like they did the other uplifted species, or just wiped you out. The betting's about even right now, but it's going to tilt pretty heavy if the galaxy ever finds out about Maximus and his gang."

"Why wouldn't they?" Gareth asked. "Don't human's stand out?"

"We were successful in turning him into a Vanir," Morty said. "*Those Left Behind* are what's left of the Chaa. When they evolved beyond material forms, only a few really wanted to go, so they took it upon themselves to become gods. Transformed the rest of their kin into the current form. But to keep them from getting lonely, so the story goes, they uplifted all the other species at the same time."

"And inhibited them from violence?" Gareth asked, making sure he had understood all the previous explanations.

"For the most part," Xiomber chimed in. "We're all bound up into a single, psionic entity. That's what the *Accord of Souls* is all about. Empathy. But some folks feel it more and some less. Those individuals who are at the low end tend to become criminals, like us."

"And we're completely outside of your empathy, so Cinnra wanted a human as an assassin," Gareth completed the thought. "Except I'm a police officer. A Field Agent with Earth Force Sky Patrol. The good guys. Shouldn't we be contacting a Vanir Constable to help them?"

"Pal, if they could stop Maximus Sarzynski, we already would have turned ourselves in and turned state's evidence. They got no chance in hell of stopping that guy. That's why we needed you."

"So now I'm a hunted criminal," Gareth observed. "And I'm supposed to help two other wanted criminals stop an entire gang of wanted criminals from taking over the galaxy?"

"You got it, pal," Xiomber cracked wise, leaning back into his seat.

"Who the hell do you think I am?" Gareth rasped.

"A hero," Morty replied in deadly seriousness.

Gareth slammed his mouth shut when it fell open. Scowled hard, but the Yuudixtl scientist was immune to his look.

And the little lizardman was right. That was all he had ever wanted to be.

A hero.

THE ARSENAL

PROFESSOR LOUGHTY MADE sure everyone else stayed at the door, including his daughter Philippa. Given his druthers, she wouldn't even be here, but his headstrong, only, daughter was not one to be easily thwarted. Especially not when her beau was the one that had disappeared.

Royston Loughty, *PhD*, *FRS*, *CBE*, *CStJ*, already thought of Gareth as his son-in-law. The young man had pressed his case early on, and then spent several years reminding Royston and Philippa of his love. But nobody and nothing could crack that man's hard head that he had to be promoted to the rank of Field Agent before he would formally propose. And Royston had tried every trick he could think of over the years.

Worse, he had known that Gareth was all prepared to finally propose, but Royston couldn't tell Pip that. She was already on the verge of tears, standing in the doorway with a fist to her mouth, the short, red shirt and tunic of a Sky Patrol Auxiliary reminding everyone how tough she was.

Royston smiled at his daughter as his portable scanner went to work. She had her mother's red hair and green eyes, rather than his own darker complexion, but Pippa had gotten her height from him, as well as his bones, in comparison to his dear-departed Elizabeth.

However, Pip had had gotten Elizabeth's strength, and her force of will, which served the young woman well, both in dealing with Gareth and her father, and also with society in general. The world frowned on a woman of science, such as Pip had become. She had earned her university degree, but no college would admit her to higher studies, so he had brought her with him to Earth Force's Headquarters in orbit where she had met and fallen madly in love with a rising agent.

Who had just vanished.

Royston would have considered the entire thing to be an elaborate practical joke, even after listening to the audio tapes of Gareth's last call, except that the portable scanner kept returning bizarre radiation signatures, no matter how he tuned it. Nothing dangerous or he would have never allowed his only daughter in here regardless of her impending engagement to the man in question.

No, just *strange*. Nothing he could explain, and he was Earth Force's preeminent expert on stellar radiation.

Something must have shown on his face.

"What is it, Father?" Pippa asked in a serious voice that still could have filled opera halls with its musicality, had she been of the mind.

"Sir?" Sector Marshal Alvin Siddall asked from over Pippa's shoulder from the hallway.

Royston found it amusing that the commander of The Arsenal itself was so deferential, but the situation was well outside anything Earth Force had ever encountered. That was why he had called in Royston. Plus, it had been Gareth. Everyone knew about that connection.

"There is something here," Royston admitted. "I cannot

explain it. However, I can see it, and thus, it must exist and be explainable. Seal the room off for now. I will need to return with better equipment."

"Where is he?" Siddall asked. "Where could Gareth go?"

Royston drew himself up fully. Like the Sector Marshal, he was over six feet tall. Unlike the other man, Royston was only a little pudgy around middle and not turning fat like the man who spent too much time behind a desk.

"I don't know, Marshal Siddell, Pippa," he acknowledged them both, especially the depths of fear in Philippa's eyes. "Nothing I know can explain a man just vanishing like that. But I will find out."

DISGUISED

GARETH LOOKED around the strange office where the flying taxi had deposited them. The room was large and airy, but mostly empty, except for a few racks of clothes near one gray wall and a couple of triple mirrors standing in the back corner on his right, plus a pair of blue couches in the middle.

Still, Morty seemed at home, and Xiomber as well. Both took seats on the one couch and gestured Gareth to the other.

Outside, the taxi dove out of sight and the balcony door closed, sealing them off from the cotton-candy skies of *Orgoth Vortai.*

"Welcome," a disembodied, male voice filled the oversized room. "What'll it be, Morty, Xiomber? You two finally ready to dress better?"

Gareth had to agree with the voice. Both lizardmen were wearing something rough equivalent to common dungarees in blue, with pull-over T-shirts, Xiomber's in black and Morty's red with the strange design on the front. Gareth felt desperately overdressed in his Field Agent uniform. The two lizardmen dressed like a couple of machinists out for a beer after work.

"Nothing so grand, Jorghen," Morty called back. "And I sure as hell wouldn't have you do my wardrobe. Need to make the Vanir here look less memorable. His name's Gareth."

Vanir? Oh, right. Not human. Short Vanir. That's the cover story. I can do that.

"Gareth?" the man asked. "Stand up and walk to the mirrors on your right."

Gareth did, nervous, but not too much. Socially awkward, maybe.

His image came back in triplicate from the nine-foot-tall mirrors. A light flashed in his eyes, and the image in the reflection was suddenly wearing black pants, baggy enough that they covered his boots instead of tucking in. The Sky Patrol tunic was gone, as well. In its place, a plain, white t-shirt, underneath a button-down, button-up shirt in Sky Patrol plaid colors. A jacket appeared over top of that after a moment, blue denim like the Yuudixtl pair's pants, with bronzed buttons and a small SP button stuck through the flap of the left breast pocket.

Hey, that wasn't bad looking.

"Why not just take him to a department store?" Jorghen's disembodied voice came from all around a moment later.

"He gets self-conscious, shopping in the kids section, Jorghen," Morty fired back. "You, of all people, should appreciate that."

Jorghen had a crude laugh. Ugly. The bully at school picking on the other kids, at least until Gareth put a stop to it. But discretion was still called for here.

"You like that, Gareth?" Jorghen asked. "The fashion's a little offbeat, but that's what your subconscious wanted."

Gareth turned a nervous eye to the two Yuudixtl scientists. Morty nodded. So did Xiomber.

"Yeah," Gareth admitted.

He couldn't remember the last time he had dressed as a civilian. It had to be before he went off to school, ten years ago. The guy in the mirror looked like a cowboy, in the good ways. Like maybe if he added a hat, he could star in Westerns. Add a seven point star and he could be the town marshal.

"Okay," Jorghen said. "Take me about thirty minutes to kick it out. You leaving the other outfit here?"

Gareth panicked. Give up my Field Agent uniform? Never.

"Uhm, no," he settled for, rather than unleashing a blistering stream of the sorts of profanities he had first learned from the enlisted Chief on his first command.

"Put it on my account, Jorghen," Morty said. "And spin him up a set of formal robes, as well. Something High Street, but without all the flash of an investment banker. Low profile, as it were. We need to be able to eat at a fancy restaurant with a dress code."

"Add about ten minutes then," the man said. "Coming right up. Have some tea while you wait."

Gareth thought about it, but he really needed to pee. More tea would make it worse.

Instead, he leaned close the two criminals.

"Uhm, I need to use the facilities," he whispered.

"Through there," Xiomber pointed.

"But…"

"Erect bipeds, Gareth," Morty said. "Same design. Find the target at your height. Simple as that."

Gareth blushed and nodded.

When he got up this morning, peeing in an alien toilet

was not anywhere on his list of things to consider. Still, he was Sky Patrol. He could do this.

The door opened easy enough. A counter with a mirror and a sink on the left. Stalls and urinals on the right. A red light came on as he stepped close to one.

Motion sensor.

Still, he managed, even with all the extra publicity. It flushed itself as he backed up and looked around.

There were no handles on the faucet.

None.

He got lucky and it went off when he passed a hand underneath.

Huh.

That was smart.

Out in the main room, the boys were sipping more tea. Gareth passed, for now. There was enough caffeine in his system for one day. And it was close to midnight, back on Earth. He would need to sleep soon.

In fact, the couch looked comfortable. He sat down, leaned back, and closed his eyes.

"WAKE UP, SLEEPY HEAD," a merry voice intruded. "You need to change and put your stuff in the bag."

Gareth climbed out of his bizarre dreams, into his bizarre reality. Hopefully this one was better.

He really didn't want to see a tentacled cow again. Like, ever.

The outfit from the mirror was hanging on hooks next to the mirror itself. Quickly, Gareth transformed himself into an Undercover Agent working a deep mission. A cowboy, even. The boots were wrong, but hopefully none of the locals would notice.

The Field Agent uniform got folded up exactly to regulation and put away, atop a piece of fabric that appeared to be a thick, soft black silk, shot through with red and cream glitter. It was the most beautiful piece of fabric he had ever seen.

"Thank you, sir," Secret Agent Gareth said to the room as he picked up and bag and slung the strap over his shoulder.

"Any time, Gareth," Jorghen said. "It's interesting, watching the machines locate the clothes you want to wear, as opposed to what society would inflict on a short Vanir."

"Let's go," Morty groused. "Time's wasting."

Out the door and onto the balcony. Another taxi settled in and opened for them. Gareth followed the little men into the cabin and leaned back, seatbelts in place.

"Now what?" he asked sleepily.

"Now we've got a little bit of a jaunt," Morty said. "Why don't you sleep for now, and we'll wake you up when we get there."

"I could never…" Gareth began to say as the day caught up with him and darkness descended.

CONSTABLE BAKER

"YOU HAVE GOT TO BE KIDDING," Constable Eveth Baker rasped into the telephonetics handset as she furiously wrote notes into an old-fashioned, leather-bound notebook with an even older-fashioned pencil.

The written word calmed her. Words on a page, rather than a screen, somehow rearranged themselves in her imagination to create new links between clues that she didn't think about consciously.

"Fine," she continued. "But you better be right, or the weekly stipend we pay you for these sorts of leads just might dry up."

Eveth slammed the handset down angrily and looked around the police bullpen where she was working. The space always felt dingy in her memory, when she wasn't here, but the room itself was clean and spacious. Well designed for calming psychology. It was just her that wanted it to reflect some of the squalor of the job.

Across the shared desk, her partner looked up from his reading with studied casualness. Senior Constable Jackeith Grodray was a by-the-book cop. The old man of the precinct they had paired her with in an effort to tone down some of the crazier things Eveth knew she did when pursuing the criminal element.

He was tall for a Vanir male, more than seven foot, two inches in stocking feet, but skinny. The man weighed barely three hundred pounds. Grodray was an intellectual cop. Divorced with two kids in school. Forty One Standard Cycles old, the light brown hair on his temples was turning gray now, and while he might have lost a step in a footrace, the Senior Constable had gotten that much better at outsmarting the bad guys so he never had to chase them down.

And he had Eveth, if it came to that. She liked pursuing criminals who thought they could get away.

Even his uniform tunic somehow conveyed the image of a staid academic, well-tailored to his overall shape with the bright, cerulean-blue ring of the *Accord of Souls* over his heart. Hers were always wrinkly and dusty, but that was the time she spent crawling under desks and into dark corners looking for clues.

"Something interesting?" her partner asked in a quiet, droll voice.

The room was mostly empty this afternoon. Quiet, save for a drunk snoring loudly in a cage in one corner of the office. Everyone else was out doing things, so they had almost the entire floor almost to themselves right now.

"One of my secret informers," Eveth shrugged and took a calming breath. Getting emotional with Grodray never did any good. The man was deduction, boiled down and decanted into a glass bottle. Emotions just washed off his narrow, sturdy chest like rain. "Usually, the man's reliable. This time, he claims that they heard rumors of a human, of all things, running loose on *Orgoth Vortai*, right here in Punarvasu."

"Again?" Grodray asked. "Haven't we had enough of these wild goose chases?"

"Get this," Eveth said. "Completely different description, this time. A pretty detailed one, at that."

She relayed everything off of her notepad slowly, letting her partner digest the words. He was all about processing things like a prospector seeking gold flakes. Swirl the water slowly, let it settle, add some more water, swirl some more. Eventually, the good stuff would settle to the bottom of the pan, once all the dross was removed.

Something caught her eye as she repeated it. Intuition snuck in and bit her on the ear, like it did.

"What?" Grodray asked as he realized she had stopped talking in the middle of a sentence.

Eveth turned her attention to the keyboard on the desk before her and typed furiously.

Suddenly, the screen flashed bright red and a beep chimed angrily at her.

WARNING. Information classified. Enter Level-7 security authorization to proceed.

"*Fardel*," she grumbled angrily under her breath.

A Constable like her was only Level-3.

"What are you trying to do, Baker?" he asked warily, standing and walking around towards her side of the desk.

She showed him the description of the clothing the human was supposedly wearing, written hurriedly as the informer had spoken.

"See?" she asked. "Red jacket. Black and gold design on the chest. I was trying to look something up about the humans that I thought I remembered, but the system wants a Level-7 clearance. Not worth trying to ask a Senior Inspector. They'll just tell me I'm imagining things."

"What are you imagining, Eveth?" Jackeith questioned quietly.

"A uniform," she said, flipping back through her notebook unsuccessfully. "Or something. It was part of a throwaway line that one Inspector made, back when they briefed us about humans during the first scare, last winter. Damn it, this notebook is too new. I'll have to look it up when I get home tonight."

"Here," Grodray said, leaning over her shoulder and typing something into the keyboard.

The screen flashed a welcome and brought up an image of a Vanir male. Except it wasn't. This was a human.

And Jackeith Grodray had typed his password into…

"How in the nine hells did you do that?" she stared up at him in surprise. "That was a Level-7 authorization."

"Uh huh," he smiled back serenely. Like always.

"But you're only a Senior Constable," she continued, confused and maybe a little frustrated. "That should only grant you Level-4, maybe Level-5 at best."

"I only ever wanted to be a Senior Constable, Eveth," he answered calmly. "Plus, I had to do some things several years ago. This was back before we were partners. They had to read me in on some very dangerous secrets."

Eveth flushed with a moment of pure avarice at the thought of the crimes you could solve with that level of clearance.

"So what have we got?" Grodray continued, still serene, damn it.

Eveth pointed at the screen, going back and forth between her notes and the image.

"White pants," she observed. "Check. Dark red tunic with weird gold things on the shoulders. Check. Black background a foot wide, center of chest, with some weird logo in gold in the middle. Check. The description also included three white rings around the black, separated by red lines."

"Three, you said?" he asked in a voice suddenly gone cold and stern.

She looked up again, feeling her face harden. It matched Jackeith's in that.

"Yes, three," she replied. "What's going on, Grodray?"

She watched him call up a menu item quickly and toggle something. The image changed, and now the chest had three rings around the black.

"The thing in the middle are two letters, Baker," he said carefully, glancing up to make sure they were still alone in the room. "From the principle language on Earth. *SP*. Stands for Sky Patrol. Part of the Earth Force that humans have over their single solar system."

"A military?" she asked, suddenly scrambling to her feet. She needed to be out on the streets, if there really was a human, a warrior, loose in this city.

"No," Grodray placated her with one hand and a calm voice. "That's the uniform of an Earth Force Sky Patrol Field Agent, Baker."

"Meaning?" she asked.

"He's a cop, like us."

UNDERWORLD

"WHAT DO WE KNOW?" Marc asked harshly as the two Warreth females entered his personal chambers.

He generally didn't like dragging everyone into the throne room, except for special occasions. That kept the mystique going. This was business.

"Got a lead, but we've got a problem, Maximus," Maiair replied.

They were sisters, Maiair and Yooyar. Primarily crimson in their feathers, with black and white highlights. Maiair was taller, but only slightly, and a year older.

Yooyar was probably the more dangerous of the two, however, the older sister was the cannier opponent.

"What happened?" Marc asked, moving across the outer chamber to grab a bottle of wine.

It wasn't worth making a scene with these two. They were loyal, and could be lethal if he needed to point them at someone needing to be disciplined. He grabbed a glass and poured some wine into it while he listened.

"Morty and Xiomber indeed found themselves a human," Maiair said. "The description fits."

"Where?" Marc looked up as the glass was full. He didn't bother offering any to the sisters. They wouldn't be here long enough to drink any, and this wasn't a social call.

"*Orgoth Vortai,*" the older sister replied. "Witness puts them in Punarvasu a couple of days ago, but they've gone dark."

"They're on the run," Marc said. "They can't get far."

"Somebody made the human," Yooyar interjected. "The Constabulary got a tip. We've spotted a pair of cops in the place where Morty and Xiomber were confirmed."

Marc swirled the glass and sniffed the bouquet as he thought. Suddenly becoming a genius was incredibly useful if he needed to solve a math or physics problem, but not in the messy, complicated tides that represented the street. Still, he could use this to his advantage.

"Follow the cops," he decided. "Keep an eye out for the two traitors and the human, but let the cops do the leg work. If we get lucky, they'll flush the trio for us and we can swoop in. If not, they'll all end up in a cell somewhere and we can take care of them."

"Second problem, boss," Maiair said. "We've been down in the lab. Morty cooked everything good. Sabotaged the controllers to fry all the panels when they completed the jump. Plus, about half the generators overloaded and functionally melted."

"How bad is it?" he asked.

"Fixable," she replied. "But it will take time to build a whole new, completely-illegal, wormhole generator. Plus, if the authorities are jumpy about humans being around, someone is going to be looking at all the parts vendors, wondering who brought him here. If we suddenly buy a lot of gear, it's likely to show up on someone's radar."

"Understood," he said. "If the cops do catch them, one of those two shits are likely to offer us up as a way to either cut their sentence, or make sure that we end up in the same cell with them."

"So what do we do?" Maiair asked.

"Let's get ahead of the curve," he replied, taking a drink as he cycled down all the branches of the new decision tree faster than anyone he had ever met could match. "Keep together the hard core of the organization. Just the twenty or so we'll need for action. Have everyone else go to ground as fast as you can shut this facility down. Assume a police raid in five minutes and wipe everything. Put the A-team on the transport and get us jumped over to *Orgoth Vortai* as a tour group."

"Why there?" Yooyar asked.

Warreth didn't have a mouth that could be used to communicate emotions, like humans did. They used the feathered headcrest instead. The younger sister was confused, but that was inexperience. She had only joined the organization barely long enough ago to meet Cinnra, before Marc supplanted the old boss. She and her sister had understood which way the winds were blowing.

She was trying to figure out which way he was moving, so she didn't put a foot wrong, rather than challenging his authority. Learning, which was good. There were still a few of Cinnra's people he would need to ease out.

Or arrange lethal accidents for.

"There is no place better than anyplace else," he explained. "But they're likely to run, so we need to be in a position to give chase. Either them or the cops. This is about being close enough to force their decision curve the way we want it."

"Oh," she said, nodding firmly.

She didn't understand, but Marc expected her sister to fill in the details once they left.

He nodded them out and drank more wine.

Having Sky Patrol here changed things. The cops just might listen, if they knew what Dankworth really represented, and Sky Patrol wouldn't give up on their prey.

He should know. Packed carefully away, he still had his old uniform.

WITNESS FOR THE PROSECUTION

"YOU'RE SURE?" Eveth asked the Borren publican of the tea house, pointing at the picture in Grodray's hands.

She and Grodray had ended up back in the office with the tea house keeper. It was a tiny space with high ceilings and little art on the walls. The door was open, but that just let them see back into the kitchen, rather than the public space.

They had printed the image of a Sky Patrol Field Agent, minus all the explanations of what the thing actually was, but even then, it was never allowed out of Grodray's immediate control.

"Indeed, officer," the man said, tapping the chest. "The design was quiet interesting. I have considered doing it as a piece of art. Could I get a copy of that?"

"No," Grodray said with quiet emphasis. "In fact, if you were to put it up, *Accord* Security might take exception. I'd rather your shop not be shut down for potentially-criminal behavior. What say you?"

"Oh," the man said.

Eveth watched the manager blush, which was always

interesting on one of the Borren. They were the standard biped design, but exceptionally tall, often nearing eight feet in the male, and over seven for a female. But they were also stick-thin. At a full six-foot-seven, Eveth probably outweighed the man, despite only coming up to his shoulder.

The eyes were large, compared to most species, with a long, flat, narrow nose, and a tiny mouth, but it allowed them to see in far lower light than most species.

And they were pacifists, as a rule. Great shopkeepers, though.

He leaned back as politely as he could, putting emotional space between himself in comfortable robes, and Eveth and her partner.

"And they left after an hour?" Eveth pressed, raising her voice just enough to keep the shopkeeper's attention.

"Indeed," he agreed. "Keelee served them, and they left a good tip."

Eveth turned to look back to the kitchen.

"Keelee," she said in a loud voice at the few employees lingering and probably listening.

One of them looked up in shock, while the others edged away. She was a young Grace. Her tentacles still weren't to their full growth yet, so not that long out of school. She turned utterly umber under the force of Eveth's gaze.

"Join us?" Eveth ordered in a polite fiction that only sounded like a question.

She had left her jacket in the car today, so her armored bodysuit with the badge over her heart was obvious. Normally, a nice tunic covered it with softer lines, but today, the harshness of the blue-gray scales stood out. As did the knee-high armored boots, the holster on her hip, and the utility belt normally hidden under the tunic. Eveth had tied back her hair, but the bangs needed to be cut. She blew one up to clear her eyes.

Next to her, Grodray still had his jacket on. It made him look diplomatic.

Eveth was here to play bad cop.

Keelee shuffled over, head hanging and tentacles nearly motionless with embarrassment. The rest of the employees made themselves scarce.

Eveth caught the girl under the chin with her right hand, lifted the face up to look at her. A few tentacles carefully explored Eveth's suit, but none made it as far as her hand.

"Two Yuudixtl, and a small Vanir?" Eveth pressed, pointing at the picture. "The Vanir dressed like this?"

"Yes, sir," Keelee answered quietly.

If anything, the young woman's blush got worse. She nearly turned brown and her pupils dilated.

Eveth played a hunch.

"Did you taste the Vanir, Keelee?" she asked quietly.

That was frequently a major *faux pas* with strangers. But if he was what Grodray thought, then the stranger might not know any better.

"Girl?" the manager bellowed.

Eveth silenced the man with a hard glance. After a moment, she stepped out of the doorway to the manager's office and pulled it shut it behind her. The Senior Constable could keep him in line.

And Grodray was a guy. He might not understand.

"You can tell me, Keelee," Eveth said carefully. "They're fugitives from justice, but you had no way of knowing that."

"I did, sir," the young woman said.

Her head would have fallen, but for Eveth holding it up. Having more than a foot of height, and the muscles to match, helped.

"What did he taste like?" Eveth asked, disguising her tone as well as she could.

Keelee didn't need to hear Eveth's disgust.

Some species knew no bounds, but Eveth had never considered anyone that wasn't a Vanir. And precious few of them.

Most men were either too timid around her, or too competitive.

But Keelee had stopped breathing.

Eveth nodded.

"He wasn't a Vanir, was he?" she asked.

"No, sir," the girl said. "I've never tasted anyone like him. So warm. So purple. So dreamy."

Shit, they really did have a human on the run in the *Accord of Souls*. And a witness.

"You can never tell anyone about him, Keelee," Eveth said. "Except me or the Senior Constable in the office. Not your family. Not your coworkers. Not your boss. If you did, and I found out, someone would have to arrest you and probably put you in jail for decades."

It was a serious threat. Eveth Baker was a serious cop making it. And a decade sounded like forever when you were twenty.

"Do you understand me, Keelee?" Eveth asked, trying to be reasonable while firm.

"Yes, sir," Keelee said. "I just couldn't help myself. I had to find a way to taste him."

Huh.

"Have you ever been that way before?" Eveth asked.

"No, sir," Keelee wailed quietly. "I've always been a good girl. I'm still a virgin."

"Well stay away from that creature and you'll be safe, Keelee," Eveth instructed. "Find yourself a good boy or girl of the Grace and make art instead."

"Yes, sir," she said. "I'm sorry."

"No, you've done well, Keelee," Eveth reassured her.

"Now we know where to start, so we can find them. But you need to keep our secret. Can I trust you?"

"Oh, yes, sir," Keelee brightened.

Eveth sent her on her way and knocked on the closed door.

The Grace were all about art. Being able to see, touch, taste, and smell with those tentacles meant they lived in the richest sensory world possible.

Eveth figured she'd go nuts in a hurry, surrounded by that level of sensory bombardment, all day every day, but she wasn't an artist. Nothing like the Grace.

No, that wasn't true. She did have an art. A passion.

Hunting down criminals and bringing them to justice.

The Senior Constable emerged a moment later, shooting the manager a significant look that probably mirrored what was on Eveth's face. Perhaps a touch more refined and polite, but no less adamantine.

She nodded and headed for the front of the shop.

Out on the sidewalk, the sun was pleasantly warm, but not enough so that Jackeith would remove his jacket.

"What did the girl tell you?" he asked as they got some privacy.

The uniforms ensured that. The Constabulary were the *Accord's* police. There were other, more dangerous agencies, hidden deeper in the shadows cast by the cops, but most people still gave them a wide berth. Eveth assumed everyone was guilty of something, however small, and could use that as leverage. She was rarely wrong.

"She confirms we have a human on our hands," Eveth said. "Alien of a type she had never tasted, anyway. I didn't tell her what he was. The manager confirmed the uniform, so we know what we're dealing with. Where do we go from here?"

"Cinnra's organization were the ones behind the last

human scare," Grodray mused. "But he's no longer in the picture, according to some sources. One theory was that he did manage to recruit a human."

"So did some other underworld organization decide to engage in an arms race?" Eveth asked. "Get their own human? But could they get a worse target than a human cop, Jackeith?"

"Maybe it wasn't random luck on their part?" he contemplated. "Maybe it was intentional?"

"Are you nuts, Grodray?"

"Let's employ deduction," he began.

Eveth knew to shut up at those words. Anything she said trying to derail her partner now would just extend the conversation that much longer. He would not be budged. Not when he got like this.

She nodded, trying not to hustle him or roll her eyes.

"Suppose Cinnra got himself a human, an assassin," Grodray pondered. "And lost control of the creature, since a human killer wouldn't necessarily only kill the people Cinnra wanted."

"Speculation, but sure," Eveth injected into the spot she was supposed to say something.

"And the human killed Cinnra," Jackeith continued. "That explains some of the upheavals and shenanigans we've had to deal with on various worlds. Turf war and maybe a new boss shaking things up."

"With you so far."

Without a single eyeroll, even.

"Who would want a human cop?" Grodray posed the million-credit question.

"Someone in Cinnra's band of criminals who wants to cover his ass?" Eveth guessed. "They would be the only sort of people who would know how to get a human, outside of some very shadowy agencies that would have never let one run around unchaperoned. And they might want someone who wanted to take the first human down, and had the human violence to do it."

"Holds water, Eveth," he said.

"*Fardel*," she replied. "That means we've got a potential race war on our hands. Two uncontrolled killers, gunning for each other, with a whole *Accord* worth of innocents potentially in the way."

"Worse," her partner noted. "I'm not sure we can tell anyone, with as flimsy as our evidence is. And if we do, they'll take it away from us in a heartbeat."

"You want to take Cinnra's gang down as hard as I do?" Eveth pressed.

"Probably more, Baker," he replied. "I know things about those bastards than you do not."

Eveth wanted to ask. So desperately wanted to know the truth. It probably included an explanation of how her partner, a lowly Senior Constable, managed a security clearance at least as high as a Senior Inspector.

But she didn't dare ask. If they trusted him that much, he had no choice but to keep quiet.

Eveth wanted that level of trust placed in her by those same people, one of these days.

First, she had to take down at least one human genocide machine.

Maybe two.

TRAVELERS

"WHERE ARE WE?" Gareth asked, still a little fuzzy from his nap. They had apparently let him sleep a while. The sun was down.

"In orbit, aboard a ferry," Xiomber replied.

"Oh," Gareth said.

And then his brain woke up with a strangled cry.

In orbit? But there were no rockets firing to wake the dead. No high-thrust run at five G's to clear the atmosphere, on the way to an orbital rendezvous with Sky Patrol Headquarters or The Arsenal.

He leaned as far forward as his seatbelt would allow and stared out the window.

Sure enough, deep space stared back.

"How?" he turned to Morty, eyes as big as grapefruits.

"The taxi took us to the ferry terminal," the Yuudixtl scientist explained. "From there, a commercial wormhole bounce to orbit. In a few minutes, we'll debark at the terminal and walk aboard a tube ferry and hop over to *Hurquar*."

"That's a planet?"

"That's a planet, Gareth," Morty reassured him. "Primarily Yuudixtl, with a bunch of Vanir and Elohynn, so we'll just kind of vanish into the crowd."

"Then what?"

"Then we talk about upgrading you to take on Maximus and save the galaxy," Xiomber said firmly.

Gareth turned to look at the other brother. He wasn't sure what *upgrade* entailed, but if that was the only way to stop Marc Sarzynski, then so be it.

Some sacrifices were always worth making.

The taxi rotated and Gareth found himself staring at the side of a gorgeous space station. It was a long torus design, a tall donut with a hole in the middle, slowly rotating as he watched.

Gareth finally realized he was in zero-g, floating but for the seatbelt holding him in place. The taxi puffed suddenly and began to ease into line with hundreds of other, similar vehicles, headed into a port in the side of the station.

Inside, the taxi reversed course suddenly and flew along the mildly-inclined deck until it found a little dock and slipped in, like an egg in a carton. Heavy, metal hands grasped the sides and a small airlock door extended.

The hatch gull-winged up and Gareth followed the two brothers into a hallway long enough that he could see the curve of the station at the upward horizon, feeling like no cowboy he had ever seen.

But he looked good.

Women's heads turned as he walked through the thin crowds, all headed towards a stairwell.

Gareth heard Xiomber whisper to Morty as they walked.

"When this is done, I got a couple of long cons we need to run, using our boy here," the lizard chuckled.

Morty joined in with him. Gareth blushed. He would be in their debt, if they helped him bring Maximus to justice.

And they had talked about doing a little swindle, so that he could help pay them back for giving up everything. That wouldn't be such a bad thing, would it?

Assuming they all managed to not be in jail when it was done.

Up a deck, Morty led them to a private booth, well off in a corner.

"Get in, sit down, shut up," Morty ordered. "I'm going to go get us some food."

"Everything good?" Xiomber asked.

"I thought getting him new clothes would make the guy less memorable," Morty shot back. "Shows what I know about women."

"I know how little you know about dames, buddy," Xiomber cracked. "Grab us some dim sum. I'll keep Gareth safe from bands of horny chicks."

Morty sighed and closed the door.

"Now what?" Gareth asked again.

He had a feeling he would be saying that a lot.

"In about thirty or forty-five minutes, the ferry will drop into a wormhole and we'll emerge on *Hurquar*," Xiomber said. "Not sure who he talked to or where we're going, but Morty's got connections everywhere."

"Why not take a personal wormhole?" Gareth asked. "Like you did me?"

"Because those are extremely illegal, highly dangerous, and incredibly expensive to operate," Xiomber replied. "If you managed to accidentally cross-connect two of them, you might vaporize half a hemisphere. Cinnra was desperate enough to build one in order to get Maximus. Morty and I were desperate enough to get you. Plus, we blew that one up when we left. And everyone travels commercial. Established corridors and times. Safe and comfortable. Was your first trip comfortable?"

Gareth shut his mouth. Xiomber didn't need to know about him screaming like a little girl lost in the forest.

"No," Gareth admitted. "Not really."

"Yeah, and multiply that by hundreds of inhabited worlds," Xiomber replied. "So everyone's inside a big, safe ferry with no outside windows unless they want to go to the observation deck."

"Huh," Gareth said. "But we're still going to stop Maximus?"

"Pal, we're going to try."

HURQUAR

IT HAD BEEN a different taxi that took them to the surface of the new planet. Gareth had been awake this time, to follow the reverse process. Undock from the little egg carton, join the stream of vehicles splitting into five different groups, apparently to transfer to five cities down on the surface.

Morty had opaqued most of the the windows, but left one for Gareth to watch.

He felt like a golden retriever allowed in the car on a winter day, nose against the glass and tail wagging.

Into a cubical zone marked by eight satellites the size of small space stations. Park briefly. Flash of gold as they rode into a hole in space.

The tube was a short ride, compared to coming here from Earth, but that made sense. How many light centuries, compared to fractions of a light second?

The sky over Olehmmishqu was closer to the blue Gareth expected. Still a little too green, and there were two small moons visible on the horizon when he looked.

The ground looked like a city.

Well, no.

On earth, the cities were either really old and organic in shape, or more modern and square as a rule.

Olehmmishqu was built on a series of interconnected hexagons. Xiomber had produced a pocketcomm and let Gareth spend most of the trip reading about the Moisa. All he could think of to compare them to was a giant praying mantis, with four arms (two primary, two delicate), and six legs coming off of a very short abdomen, like a weird centaur or something.

They built hexagonally, in memory of the great nests they had established before being uplifted.

Gareth had a hard time imagining a flightless bumblebee, but that was sort of the niche they had filled on *Ticcia* and brought with them into the galaxy, like at *Hurquar*.

They apparently made fantastic architects. Gareth could see that, looking down at the various buildings, laid out like a map from above. The towers and such were every shape under the rainbow, and every color he'd ever considered. Or something like that.

This was all still a little weird, even for a Field Agent of the Sky Patrol.

But eventually, the taxi brought them to the roof of a mid-sized building, kinda sorta near the south(?) edge of town. It was cold up here. Gareth was glad he had the denim jacket, although he would need something heavier if they got into winter on some planet.

And a raincoat.

This was an advanced, galactic civilization. Couldn't they do something about weather control?

The elevator wasn't a box. It was a hollow tube. Morty stepped into air like a coyote accidentally running off a cliff chasing a road runner.

"Level forty-seven," he said and then vanished.

"You next," Xiomber prompted.

Gareth peeked over the edge of the hole to see a rapidly-receding Yuudixtl scientist.

Sure. Free-fall and trust the building to catch you. What happens if the power goes out?

Gareth gulped. He had an audience, and this was no time to ask for a stairwell. He gritted his teeth and stepped forward.

Something held his foot, but he didn't dare look down to see what.

Just pretend you know what you're doing.

"Level forty-seven," he said, maybe a little louder than necessary.

He plummeted, but there was no feeling of wind. It was like he was in his own, little cocoon. Thirty-three stories raced by faster than he could count, and then he was magically standing on the deck, next to Morty.

The little lizard's knowing grin broke the ice around Gareth's soul.

"Fun?" Morty asked.

"Efficient," Gareth countered, thinking back to the times he had to take a lot of stairs because there were too many people trying to use too few elevators.

When he got home, he was going to have to find a way to invent these elevators. Or hire a Moisa architect to rebuild The Arsenal.

Xiomber was there a moment later, grinning as well.

Huh. Yuudixtl didn't really have lips like humans did. The grin was there in the eyes and the way the skin around them pulled tight and folded in. And the jaw dropped open just a shade.

Maybe he had spent enough time around the brothers to understand the non-verbal communication better. It had been two and a half days now.

Or maybe the magic PBJ sandwich was still modifying his brain. There was always that.

Morty suddenly walked forward, drawing the other two into his wake.

Gareth squinted at the writing on the door where they stopped, and suddenly the letters transformed into something he could read.

Biomimetics Heavy Southern Industries LLKR didn't make any sense, though. Maybe a cultural thing?

Morty went in, so Gareth followed, through a boring reception area into a bigger space.

Now this was a mad scientist lab. Beakers, burners, racks of tubes arranged on black, heavy workbenches. It even smelled mad, with that cloying hint of ammonia he always associated with danger in a laboratory.

There was a Nari standing across one of the black-topped desks, writing on a white board with some sort of electronic pen. She was making adjustments to an animated image as he watched.

She turned, and locked eyes with Gareth. And smiled.

Gareth felt uncomfortable, like he was back at the teashop, but this one might not settle for just sniffing him.

"Heya, Talyarkinash," Morty said, circling the tall desk.

The beautiful woman finally broke the stare and Gareth remembered to breathe. And start walking again.

Xiomber rolled his eyes when Gareth glanced down, but the little scientist kept quiet.

Hey, it wasn't his fault.

"So what have you brought me this time, Morty?" Talyarkinash seemed to purr, glancing back in Gareth's direction.

He stayed on this side of the big workbench, just in case.

She was just gorgeous, even if she was a bipedal lynx with upright ears and whiskers. Bright cobalt eyes complemented a resplendent pelt in what Gareth thought of as Imperial Blue. He had had a cat that silver-blue shade when he was young. He found himself clenching at the thought of this one also climbing into his lap and kneading.

She had that look in her eyes.

Yup, staying over here.

"Talyarkinash, this is Gareth Dankworth," Morty introduced them, shaking her hand and then pointing.

Xiomber also got a polite shake.

Then she turned and stepped close enough to the workbench to hold out her hand.

Gareth took it gingerly, watching her nostrils flare and her eyes slit, just the tiniest amount.

"Already got a Nari girlfriend?" she asked.

Purred, maybe?

"Huh?" Gareth managed, losing himself in those deep eyes.

"Knock it off, Talyarkinash," Morty chided her. "Random dame on the slidewalk literally handed him a scent card out of the blue yesterday. You still got it with you kid?"

"Huh?" Gareth managed to repeat. "Oh. Yeah."

He pulled out his wallet and extracted the card, holding it up, but not out. It was his card and he was keeping it.

But he could smell the other woman's perfume on it. Or her musk.

Uncomfortable here.

"So she doesn't have a claim?" the cat woman asked silkily.

Claim?

"Uhm, not really?" Gareth supposed.

"Good," Talyarkinash said. "So what can I do for you? Or to you?"

Gareth carefully stuck the card back in his wallet as an

excuse to look down. He was sure his face had turned the color of his hidden uniform right now.

"So, you remember that project we hired you for, about five months ago?" Morty asked delicately.

"Sure," the woman said. "You needed me to modify an alien. Brought me another one?"

Gareth did NOT like that gleam in her eyes when he looked up again. He held his breath and considered if he should just find a cop and try to explain everything, in spite of what the brothers had warned him would happen at that point.

He was not supposed to be a criminal. It went against everything Earth Force Sky Patrol stood for.

But he wasn't a Field Agent here. No, this was time to be a *Secret Agent*.

Gareth held his calm. He hoped. The way her nostrils kept working suggested that she was studying him far closer than a casual acquaintance in a lab.

"Gareth is a human," Xiomber said baldly.

That helped.

Talyarkinash stepped a whole pace back from her edge of the desk, and her ears rotated in different directions: one still pointed at Gareth, and the other now locking in on Morty.

Gareth felt better. Maybe she wasn't about to make unusually-personal suggestions now.

"You brought one of *them*?" she snarled. "Here?"

"Another one," Morty snapped back at the woman, reminding her.

She was twice Morty's size, and really angry right now, but the two brothers almost looked like they were challenging her to say or do something stupid.

Who knew what a pair of Yuudixtl scientists could do against a Nari?

The woman retreated another step but otherwise held her ground. And her peace.

"Maximus is a human," Morty continued. "Or was before you. I'm not sure quite what he is these days. You upgraded the physical to a Vanir. And Xiomber and I did the mental afterwards."

"Bastards," she hissed. "You brought a human into my lab? Do you want to get me shut down?"

"No," Morty said. "I want your freaking help making Gareth here at least a match for Maximus, before that bastard takes over the whole criminal underworld, and then follows that up by taking over the entire *Accord of Souls*. You think that sort of thing's going to help business?"

"You think a race war is going to help?" she snapped angrily. "Two them hunting each other through the planets? I might be shady, but I'm not going to be party to mass casualties of innocents, Morty. You can take your business elsewhere right now."

"He's a cop, Talyarkinash," Xiomber added.

"And you brought a cop into my lab?" she growled. "What in the nine hells is wrong with you people?"

"It's the only way to stop Maximus," Morty said simply. "Nobody but a human has the necessary violent tendencies *and* lacks the psionic resonance of the *Accord*."

"You're a cop?" she sneered at him.

Gareth felt like she was sizing him up for a physical assault now, rather than an emotional one. But that was the sort of thing he could deal with.

Even if he had to let a woman hit him first. Hopefully, she wasn't that strong.

It would probably still hurt.

"My name is Gareth St. John Dankworth," he explained slowly, enunciating each syllable. "I am a Field Agent of the Earth Force Sky Patrol. Like Morty said, an officer of the law.

Marc Sarzynski, the man you know as Maximus, is a renegade agent with a bounty on his head, back on Earth. And I will see him returned to Earth and brought to justice."

"Back on Earth?" she scoffed, before turning to the two lizardmen. "You haven't told him, have you?"

"Told me what?" Gareth felt his stomach go cold.

"No," Morty said acidly. "We hadn't. Not yet. That was supposed to come later, but I guess we'll have to cover it now. Thank you, by the way."

"I did owe you one, for bringing a cop in here."

"Told me what?" Gareth focused on Morty and Xiomber now.

"No Earthman knows about the *Accord of Souls*, Gareth," Morty explained. "Such knowledge is forbidden, because humans are the single most dangerous species known. But you're here now, and you already know too much."

"Meaning?"

"Meaning you can never return to Earth," Xiomber said, possibly with a wistful trace.

Gareth felt his vision go gray. Something was wrong with his balance and both hands slammed heavily onto the top of workbench, catching his weight.

Never go home?

Never see his friends and crew again?

Never hold Philippa in his arms again? Unable to propose to her? Marry her? Start a happy life as man and woman?

For the briefest moment, rage threatened to overcome him. To make these two, these three, pay for what they had taken away from him forever.

Gareth sucked a breath deep into his soul and focused on the far wall.

The Nari woman had backed up another step, ears back and eyes showing white around the edges.

Gareth suspected he looked like all their worst nightmares brought to flesh before them. He certainly felt like it.

But Marc Sarzynski was here. Running loose in the wider galaxy. Who knew what terrible grief the universe would come to if that man wasn't stopped.

And they had upgraded him, whatever that meant. These three people, he suspected, held all the guilt at such work.

What was it Xiomber had said? Only humans could be genetically engineered to go beyond the limits placed on everyone else by the Chaa?

Marc had always been a fantastic athlete back at Earth Forces Institute. He and Gareth frequently alternated first and second with everyone else vying for a distant third.

Academics had been the same way, with only three thousandths of a point finally separating them on graduation. It was one of the few times Gareth had actually been better, however thin that razor.

And then Deputy Agents with the Sky Patrol.

And Philippa.

She had chosen Gareth, and something had died in Marc Sarzynski. Turned him to darkness. Got him cast out of the Sky Patrol one short step ahead of his arrest.

And then he disappeared, until Gareth came that close to catching him in the process of breaking up a band of smugglers and slavers operating out of the UnderHives of Mars.

To apparently come here, to the *Accord of Souls*.

Gareth hoped it wasn't all a fever dream leading his subconscious over the rainbow.

Another breath.

Gareth forced his fists to unclench, noting how nervous the two Yuudixtl were in addition to the Nari woman.

Yes, he was capable of devastating violence. They all were. It was part of what made humans what they were.

And why Earth Force needed the Sky Patrol.

"He's here, and he must be stopped," Gareth finally said heavily, eyeing each of them individually. "Whatever the cost."

"Are you sure?" Xiomber asked. "We might could somehow try and erase a chunk of your memory instead, if we got lucky."

"Whatever the cost," Gareth repeated.

PART TWO

HUNTERS

EXAMINATION

GARETH STUDIED the secret lab Talyarkinash had taken him to. They had passed through a door hidden by a swinging bookcase, gone down a level, and entered into a smaller space that reminded him more of a dentist's office than anything else.

The scents in here were almost nothing, layered over with floral hints and something subtle his brain kept wanting to interpret as Talyarkinash herself. Recessed lights filled the room with bright white illumination.

One wall was a glass window that felt heavy enough to stop bullets when Gareth had tapped it.

She and the two lizardmen had gone through another door and sealed it up tight behind them. They were on the other side of that glass now, watching him intently.

"First, I'll need to scan you, Gareth," the Nari woman said over a speaker. "Please make yourself comfortable in the chair and let it adjust itself to your body."

Dentist chair. Mad Scientist Dentist's chair.

Xiomber had said that a male Vanir could be over seven

feet tall, with the females close behind. This chair would fit them.

For once, he actually felt rather like a juvenile Vanir, by comparison.

But he climbed in. Let the cold leather warm slowly against his back, with his jacket and flannel shirt hanging on a hook by the door. He had only the tight, white, t-shirt against the chill, but that cold was in his soul.

The air in the room was a pleasant seventy degrees.

Slowly, the chair moved. Gareth would have jumped up, but she had warned him.

It seemed to shrink under him, adjusting and accommodating until it fit like a hammock.

After a moment, it tilted itself back, giving Gareth a view of a device hanging from the ceiling that was in no way something so simple as the X-ray machine to take pictures of his teeth.

"Ready?" the woman asked nervously.

She sounded more emotional than he felt right this moment, but Gareth supposed she was expecting a Viking Berserker to break loose in her lab. He just needed to get this over with so he could go out and hunt down the man who had once been his fiercest rival.

And his best friend.

"Ready," Gareth said.

"I'll need to hold you in place while I scan you, Gareth," she reminded him for the fourth time. "Tell me when you are comfortable."

"Go ahead," he called, holding all his emotions tight inside.

They were long since past the time to panic. Or to stop.

Gareth locked all his muscles as the dentist's chair seemed to unfold itself a second time. Metal bars slid over his wrists and shins, binding them tight against the chair. Another strap crossed his chest, and a helmet lowered itself to cover most of his head, leaving only his mouth and part of his nose uncovered.

He wasn't claustrophobic, but the feelings weren't that far away right now.

"This is only supposed to tickle, Gareth," she said over the intercom. "Please let me know if you start experiencing pain."

"Will do," he said.

Ants. Walking across his skin but not biting. The leaves of a weeping willow as he walked through them. The cool chill of a morning fog as he jogged around the track, back at the Institute, watching the sun come up higher on every lap.

A bright light passed through his eyelids and bored a tunnel into his mind like a three-quarter inch bit being driven by a three-quarter-horse-power motor.

Gareth ground his teeth together and refused to make a sound.

"Everything okay?" Xiomber asked. "Vital signs just jumped."

"Sharp, but controllable," Gareth called back, willing everything to stillness again. "Keep going."

Hunt the man down. Bring him to justice, whatever that looked like here.

Whatever the cost.

The ants were biting now. Nasty, Texas fire ants pouring acid into his veins. The willow was a rose bush, slashing him with thorns. The fog was an icy pond he had just fallen into, through the ice.

Whatever the cost.

Something changed in his brain. The pain was there, but pushed to one side. He could think through it, or at least around it. Gareth focused his will, pushed, and the pulsing turned outward, as though he was somehow driving the drill bit backwards and closing the hole up, faster than the machine could tunnel.

Everything let go so suddenly Gareth thought he would pass out.

The pain was gone. The fire. The cold. Everything.

The chair let go and moved him more or less upright.

Gareth swung his feet over and stood up, only wobbling slightly.

"How are you doing in there?" Morty asked carefully.

"Headache," he replied. "But it's going away now.

"You had pain?" the woman asked. "It's not supposed to do that."

"I overcame it," Gareth growled. "What's next?"

"Come in here and we'll watch the readouts," she said. "It will only take a few minutes to process everything."

The door unlocked noisily and swung open on silent hinges. Gareth stepped through into a sound studio.

One long console sat under the window, filled with hundreds of gauges, knobs, and sliders. Gareth had no idea what it all did, but he recognized the human outline on a large monitor beside the window.

The writing on the screen was mostly words he could make out, but Gareth was completely lost as to what they said.

He took a chair in a far corner and concentrated on breathing and reducing his heart rate.

It felt like he had just run from Marathon to Athens in a single instant.

A machine spit out a long strip of paper, clucking to itself like a hen.

Talyarkinash was studying the readout, holding it low enough for Morty and Xiomber to read it as well.

Someone whistled, low and startled.

Gareth looked up and studied the three scientists.

"Gareth," she said carefully. "Where would you say you rank, in terms of expressed, human potential?"

It took him three tries to process her words into something that made sense.

"Probably near the top, in terms of mental, physical, and emotional," he replied through his exhaustion. "Sky Patrol Institute is a grueling test that lasts four years. I graduated at the top of my class. Marc Sarzynski was a very close second."

"You went to school together?" She was aghast.

"I told you that."

"I thought that meant you knew of him," she countered. "How close were you?"

"He would have been my best man at my wedding, one of these days," Gareth said firmly. "Now I'll see him buried under the jail, if it's the last thing I do. Why?"

"So we scanned him then, but not to the level we just did with you," Morty explained as the Nari woman fell mute. "Plus, I know roughly where we put him, so I was looking for what we could do to improve you. We'll probably only get one shot to do it, and I want to get all we can. You'll be facing both Maximus and the Constabulary at the same time. Neither will play nice."

"So what did you learn?" Gareth felt some level of anxiety creep into his voice.

"It's just that…" Morty's voice tailed off.

Xiomber stepped up and gave Gareth a level gaze.

"What he's trying to say, I presume diplomatically, is that you appear to be using fourteen percent of your expressed, genetic potential, Gareth," Xiomber said. "For comparison sake, members of the *Accord* are generally fixed at right around ninety-eight percent. We can tinker with ourselves, but nothing significant."

"Meaning?" Gareth asked. He was tired, sore, and his head hurt.

"Meaning we were able to turn Sarzynski into a genius-level Vanir, Gareth," Talyarkinash explained. "But we stopped there because we apparently didn't dream any bigger."

Genius-level Vanir.

Seven feet tall. Three hundred, twenty-five pounds of hard muscle, trained to be as dangerous as an Agent of the Sky Patrol could be. With an IQ of two hundred.

And that was dreaming too small?

"How big should we dream?" Gareth finally asked.

THE ARSENAL

ROYSTON PULLED the ticker-tape readout from the side of his radiation scanner, made a note, and scrolled backwards on the tape nearly three feet to another set of results. Briefly he wondered if the radiation machine was broken.

Or if he had tuned it too sensitive and it was reacting to just the movement of the air at this point.

Except, Gareth's room was the only place where the readings changed. Royston looked around, but nothing was out of the ordinary. The place was as standard and regulation as they came, which was to be expected of Gareth. His pocketcomm was still sitting on the desk, next to a book the young man had apparently been reading when the emergency happened. The bed tucked tight, except where he had pulled the covers slightly while sitting on them.

Uniforms all arranged in the drawers and closet exactly according to specification.

Royston had even scanned both chester and closet, on the possible chance that Gareth had brought something home with him from a recent mission, but nothing reacted.

No, the only time the machine pinged at all was when he

pointed the detector at the telephone's handset, or at a spot in the middle of the floor, almost in the center of the triangle between bed, dresser, and closet. And in both of those, the radiation reading went off the charts. It made no sense at all.

Royston turned the machine off and moved to the door. He opened it and looked out at his daughter, patiently waiting on a chair just outside.

"Any news?" she asked as she looked up.

"No," he replied. "Come inside, please, Pippa. I want to review what I've learned."

She rose with all the grace of her mother and flowed past him, holding a book of Tacitus written in Latin that she had been reading while she waited.

Closing the door, he found her seated on the one chair.

"I don't know how to tell you this, Pippa," he began.

"I'm made of far sterner stuff than you think, Father," she replied with a primness she inherited from dear Elizabeth.

"If I believed in angels and devils, I would have to only presume that one such opened the fabric of space/time itself and grabbed him," Royston said. "But since we know that to be impossible, I'm at a loss."

"Why do you presume the impossibility of such a thing, Father," she asked, eyes glaring. "In science, you have always taught me that we use deduction to eliminate the obvious, and thus, what remains, no matter how far-fetched, must be the explanation."

"Gareth Dankworth disappeared from this room in a way I cannot explain. And did so without opening any doors ," Royston said. "The air vents are too small to admit anything larger than a mouse. But he is absolutely gone."

"Then your understanding of physics are insufficient," Pippa stated flatly.

"What?"

"As you said, science cannot explain it, and yet it

happened," she retorted. "Ergo, our knowledge of science is too rudimentary to explain that angel or devil and how they were able to open a portal through space and time to kidnap Gareth. Prior to Newton, we were still bound by the laws of gravity, even though we could not explain them. Gareth was here, and then he was not. The door did not open and there is no other method of egress. Therefore, something opened a different type of portal, one we do not understand. What did your radiation detector find?"

"Something my simple understanding of physics cannot explain," Royston said, granting her the warmest smile the chills in his heart would allow.

Indeed, sterner stuff than he gave her credit. Stronger than many of the men he knew.

She was like Elizabeth in that. He missed his wife less, knowing how well their daughter had turned out.

"Tell me," Pippa commanded, Queen of England facing down the Armada.

"There is a signal when I scan the handset," Royston said, moving to the middle of the room. "The only other place I find it is here. I have scanned countless other places and rooms, and only here do I find that signature."

"What does that tell us, Father?" Pippa continued. "It tells me that Gareth was talking on the telephone when this indescribable portal opened, right where you are standing. It pulled him through before he could resist, then the handset fell. The radiation only touched those two places, as you said."

"But how did someone open a rift in space and time itself, in order to kidnap the man?" Royston asked.

"No," Pippa stated flatly. "There is a more important question we should be asking. Namely, why did they want Gareth?"

BR'ER RABBIT

"IT HELPS that the perp is so damnably memorable," Eveth said, turning away from the foot traffic on the street to study the scowl on Grodray's face.

"I agree," her partner conceded. "But now things will get interesting."

Jackeith began to walk, so Eveth fell into stride beside him.

They were at the star ferry office downtown. Had just left, headed back to their own precinct building. The sun was clouded over, giving the day a soft and uncertain taste.

"How so?" Eveth asked. "We know they made it off-planet using the ferry."

"We suspect," Grodray corrected her. "We've got a witness putting them in an auto-car in the right time window. Records show that car deposited them at a haberdashery nearby. You haven't called the operator of the shop, because we don't want to tip our hand, and to get a warrant would require that we tell someone important what we think is going on, but more of your witnesses confirm the car's arrival."

"I've got a gut feeling on this one, Grodray," Eveth said.

"And I have learned to trust your intuition, Eve," he replied. "But all a raid gets us at this point is confirmation of who was there, and maybe an actual picture of the...*perp*."

They were on a public street. Not even her by-the-books partner would use the word *human* here, for fear of starting a riot.

"What's next?" she asked, knowing his penchant for deduction.

"So the next step was tracking auto-cars from the haberdasher," he said. "Once you had the building identified, I went off and tracked outbound cars, assuming that they think they are safe. Pretty sure I found a target. Certainly, the credit account they are using belongs to a Warreth insurance salesman living on the southern coast. He'll be in for a surprise when he gets his monthly bill, unless we warn him ahead of time. That also gives too much away."

"It does," Eveth said. "I don't want to share this one bit more than I have to. Any judge we tell is going to call a Senior Inspector in."

"They will, at the very least. That's wherein the problem lies," Grodray said. "Based on what we've run down today, all the other cars that left that address over the next two hours are accounted for, except for three that went to the orbital boost for the ferry, first stop: *Hurquar*. We have to presume they caught a ride up to space, and then left the system."

"And walked right out of our jurisdiction," Eveth grumbled.

"Perhaps," Grodray countered. "Is it worth raising a fuss now?"

"Have you got the jets to lift this one, Grodray?" Eveth asked suddenly. "You've got a Level-7 Security Authorization."

"And I am very careful about how I use it, Baker," he

replied. "I can go to a judge and fill out a probable cause request. That gets us a warrant to access the haberdasher's records, but any judge we ask is likely to put in a call to a Senior Inspector, possibly the Command Inspector herself, and ask for clarification. That starts an avalanche of questions."

"In for a penny, in for a pound," she stated her position. "I want what you have. I want to be on the inside of some of those investigations you obviously can't talk about around me because I'm only Level-3. And if we've got a human loose, maybe *another* human loose, then I absolutely want to be in on that takedown."

"Even if it means being stuck running to get coffee for a Senior Inspector?" he asked. "Just being on the back of the stage while the big shots get all the credit for the work you did? The sweat you gave? The blood you shed?"

Something in his eyes told Eveth that Jackeith Grodray had been there. Had done exactly that. And let the politicians have all the credit.

But it also made him very quietly a Level-7. Almost the top of the ladder. Hunting renegade humans would be at that level.

"We are the law, Grodray," she growled. "I would rather see justice done than worry about getting my face in the newspaper."

"In that case, we need to split up," he said in all seriousness. "I'll go make a few personal calls and get things rolling. You go home and pack some clothes for a sudden, extended vacation."

She stopped cold and grabbed his arm to halt him. One hand indicated her uniform, even minus the outer tunic he was wearing.

"This uniform, this badge, is all I need, Grodray," she said.

"No, Eve," he replied. "Where we might be going, that sort of thing will get you killed."

Eveth studied the calm certainty in his eyes and let go of his arm. There was only one place that her uniform would be a hindrance. A liability.

If they were going undercover, into the very shadows where folks like Cinnra hid.

DREAMS

IT WAS something like Chinese take-out, on an alien world that had never heard of China, or dim sum. Still, it fit the bill, more or less. White, cardboard-like boxes, filled with a variety of things that had the textures of meat, or vegetables, or fish. Half a dozen bowls of sauce, arranged on the workbench on front of Gareth from sweet to hot, according to his palate. The Nari woman preferred things less salty, and the two Yuudixtl were looking for better *umami*. Whatever that was.

Gareth had a low-sided bowl in front of him, and had learned to snag a quick sample and eat it before pouring more out. So far, he was batting better than average for taste, as long as he didn't ask what anything was.

He was quite confident he didn't want to know.

The smells, however, kept him eating.

Talyarkinash sat directly across from him as she ate, watching him like a hawk. He couldn't tell if she was still interested in him or fearful. Probably both, if her ears moved the same way a Terran cat's did.

Morty was next to her. Xiomber was on this side. Both

were face-down, shoveling in food as fast as they could chew. Gareth was actually tasting his food.

"What are the established capabilities of genetic engineering in the *Accord of Souls*?" Gareth finally asked the table, unsure who would answer.

All three took turns staring at each other, hoping someone else would go first. They had been that way all afternoon.

Gareth had decided it was finally time to wrestle with the eight-hundred-pound gorilla.

"What answers are you looking for, Gareth?" Talyarkinash finally asked,

"I realize the first question I want to ask is too open-ended," he replied. "As you said earlier, the limits might be in our imagination and not in your science. Could you undo it later?"

"Undo it?" Morty asked. "Kid, we're grappling with the need to maybe make you over into a god, for lack of a better term. The most powerful being since the Chaa left. You want to give that up?"

"Morty, you're talking about making me something God never intended me to be," Gareth said. "I get that. But if you can make me into a Vanir, could you reset me to a human later? Could you possibly undo what you did to Marc?"

"Crap, Gareth," Xiomber joined in. "Nobody's ever wanted to downgrade. This has always been about trying to work our way around the Chaa's limits and not die in the process."

"I'm not a god, Morty, Xiomber," Gareth said. "I went to Sunday School when I was a kid, and there's only one God."

"First off, up until very recently, humans had lots of gods, kid," Xiomber said with authority. "Some of your cultures still do, from what research I did when we went looking for Maximus. So maybe you need a better pantheon."

"I need to know that we can undo it," Gareth was firm. "I can settle for being a hero out here. That's all I ever wanted to be. But making myself over into a monster just to fight Marc, makes me just as bad as him."

"There are no humans in the *Accord*, Gareth," the Lynx woman pointed out. "Maximus is a Vanir now, by both scope and genetics. He could breed true with a Vanir woman."

"And if you also make me one, like you plan, you've forever taken away from me the only woman I've ever loved," Gareth replied, trying to hold the heat and anger in, at least as much as possible.

"Who is she?" Talyarkinash asked carefully.

Gareth stewed for a moment and then reached for his wallet. The scent card was still there. But so was a picture he pulled out and handed to the woman criminal scientist.

"Philippa Adeline Loughty," he said. "Pippa. A human woman I've been in love with for many years. I was just about to go see her and finally propose when someone opened an illegal, cataclysmically-dangerous, private wormhole and upended my entire life. If I'm a Vanir, we can never have kids. Never raise a family. Nothing. That's what you'll have taken away from me."

"Gareth, you can never go back to Earth," Morty said. "You know that."

"You don't know that, Morty," Gareth anguished. "Like Xiomber said, maybe you'll be able to completely wipe my memory, one of these days and just deposit me back at the Arsenal like nothing happened, except for a hole in my memory."

"Would she wait for you? Talyarkinash asked.

"Yes," Gareth stated categorically, thumping the tabletop with a finger. "She already has, because I wanted to wait all these long years until I made it to Field Agent. If she disappeared, I'd wait for her."

"Wow," the woman murmured.

The others fell silent. Gareth listened to his heart pound, sure they could hear it as well.

Gareth poured a cluster of purple things that looked like barbeque pork slices onto his plate and added a dollop of the yellow sauce from the middle. It wasn't mustard, but that wasn't pork, either.

He was eating ashes, either way.

"I have an idea," the Nari said quietly. "I don't know if it would work, but it might be worth a try. Gareth, what do you know about biomimetics?"

"I'm not even sure how to spell it, Talyarkinash."

"It's a study of natural creatures and how evolution has produced various biological solutions to mechanical needs that we can mimic, shaving off development time in prototyping and adapting things," she tried to explain.

Gareth listened, but the words went over his head.

"Modifying spiders to make their webbing super strong so we can use it as thread. Or inserting useful vitamins directly into milk in the cow. That's our cover here. The lab upstairs does a little work, but mostly it's a front for money laundering and giving people new lives by modifying their face and genes to hide from cops."

"Okay?" Gareth asked.

"I'm frightened with the raw potential that humans have for manipulation," she said. "But also a little excited. We absolutely need to make you over into a Vanir just so you can hide in plain sight afterwards, but maybe we can limit the major modifications by using biomimetics as a basis."

"Did any of that make any sense to you?" Gareth asked the two Yuudixtls.

"She's talking about building you toys, Gareth," Xiomber

finally said. "Baking all the powerful enhancements into biologically-powered genetic systems that you could maybe undo later. Or at least turn off."

"That true?" he turned back to the woman.

Excitement brought out the beauty in those tanzanite eyes. Brought it back, and pressed the underlying fear of a berserker loose in her lab to the back. Mostly.

Probably about as good as it was getting for now.

"More or less," she said. "The possibilities are absolutely a blank page. I'm not even sure where I want to start. But I can turn you into a pseudo-god, with a little effort."

"Dream bigger," Gareth said.

Morty and Xiomber turned to him, jaws agape. Hers fell open a moment later.

Gareth just fixed them with a hard gaze.

"Whatever it is, you're already thinking too small," Gareth said.

He drew his inspiration from the two scientists across from him. Two criminals that were responsible for him being here, but were also going to give him the chance to stop Maximus and make it all right.

Two hard-headed Yuudixtl that reminded him of dreams from when he was a kid.

If he could not go home, he could still become a hero. He would just never allow them to make him a God. Mom and Dad wouldn't stand for that level of arrogance from their oldest child. Pastor Jacob would cast him from the kirk. And rightly so.

"I've met Nari and Grace," Gareth said. "Seen Vanir and Elohynn, Borren and Moisa, at least at a distance. Yuudixtl, however, give me an idea. I could look it up, but I'm pretty sure the Chaa didn't do it, or the Yuudixtl would have turned out differently."

"What are you babbling about, Gareth?" Morty sputtered.

"You're going to make me over into a Vanir," Gareth conceded. "I get that, since the only other choice I could see easily made would be an Elohynn, but I don't want to have to deal with wings all the time, as cool as that might be, and every kid's fantasy when they're eight."

Talyarkinash started to say something, but Gareth cut her off, even as rude as it was when a woman was talking.

"You're building me tools?" he asked her, eyes boring in. "Weapons that I'll need to fight Maximus and his gang? Going to make me a god, according to the old stories?"

She nodded, apparently breathless with anticipation.

Gareth shook his head firmly. Locked eyes with Xiomber first, and then Morty before returning to her.

"No," he told her firmly. "I want you to make me a dragon."

THE HUNTER

MARC REALIZED he had finally been in the *Accord of Souls* long enough to learn the patterns of a multi-species population, but cities as *things* never really changed. Olehmmishqu, on *Hurquar*, was really no different than New Metropolis, or reborn Shangdu, north of the ancient capitals of Nanking and Peking.

People were people, regardless of shape, color, or religious affiliation.

He was surrounded now by an entire restaurant full of them, unknowingly sharing their air with the single most wanted person in the *Accord*, at least until more people heard about Gareth Dankworth. After all, Marc was a cipher, a Vanir with a shady past working in the shadows of crime. Dankworth was still the thing parents warned their children against, human.

The man couldn't hide for long.

Marc sipped a glass of wine and studied his three dinner companions. The two Warreth sisters, the crimson raptors Maiair and Yooyar, were part of his inner circle for this mission. Zorge, the Nari scientist/spy, took the other spot.

Marc might have brought others, but these three were fitting well into his needs, and some of the others might be a little too well known to openly dine at a fancy joint like this.

And Marc really had a hankering for a good ribeye steak, something close enough to a baked potato, and a slice of pie afterwards. Gareth was out there, but he could wait. Marc knew how this city flowed.

Money went to the nice places. Here, that meant down on the river that ran slowly along a park-like Promenade. At least for the younger set. If your wealth was established and generational, you had a place up on the hills to the west.

Both were places he didn't really want to see. The two traitors wouldn't have ended up there, even trying to hide from him.

No, he needed to look in the rougher places. The warehouse district, out at the edge of town, where miles of identical blocks held tomorrow's stock in trade. Or the meat-packing district, where refrigerated transports from various farming counties and planets coalesced with their exotic products, feeding their stock to the middlemen that served the boring, banal, cultural backbone of the *Accord*: the middle classes with their presumptions and small-minded ways.

Marc needed to be down with the bohemians, the artists, and the hustlers if he wanted to find a man trying to hide. The places where crime could be contained, and concealed, but still readily ignored for a good enough bribe to the right people.

Not the Constabulary. Those people had no sense of commerce. But they also weren't that thick on the ground. No, Marc preferred the local beat cops. The men and women who knew their neighborhoods and would overlook the petty crimes for a little money on the side, as long as you kept a lid on your activities and the only victims were outsiders.

Always protect the neighborhood. Being in Olehmmishqu was really just like being home in Little Krakow, back in New Metropolis.

"What have we learned?" Marc turned his attention to Zorge, seated directly across and just finishing his salad with a crunch.

The older scientist also had the best manners of anyone Marc had kept when he thinned out some of the less-loyal elements. Zorge paused, set his fork down, dabbed at his mouth with a napkin, and sipped a bit of water.

Most of Marc's crew probably didn't know which of the forks on the table did what. At least the sisters had learned quickly when Marc told them what they needed to do to get ahead.

"I'm working on one fundamental assumption that you should pause and reconsider," Zorge said, at once vague and specific. "You are now seven foot two. Dankworth is only six foot one, from what you've said, and thus will stand out as a very short Vanir, anywhere he goes. My presumption is that Morty and Xiomber, being geneticists, will want to do the same thing to him as they did to you, possibly with a five percent increase in his physical capabilities, if that's possible."

"That was my thought, as well," Marc agreed. "I don't see him becoming an Elohynn, as interesting as the symbolism of that would be."

"Sir?" Maiair asked, obviously a little lost at the turn of phrase.

"Back home, one could make the case for me as the *Fallen One* of one of our primary religions," Marc said. "An angel who was cast out of heaven. A man who would rather rule in hell than serve in heaven. Giving Gareth Dankworth wings would make him over into Michael, the warrior archangel. Rather fitting, all things considered, but not worth discussing at this time."

"Right," Zorge said. "But that brings me to a possible logical fallacy. Would he try to outthink us by turning himself into a Nari, or a Grace? He could walk right up to this table, disguised, and none of us would be the wiser."

"I don't think so," Marc said, racing the newly-enlarged confines of his mind back over the years he had spent next to the man who had once been his best friend and greatest rival. "His ego would never let go of being human, so he'll want to stay as close as possible to that baseline. Vanir are the best place to look."

"Good," Zorge looked relieved. "I have my teams out pounding the pavement, looking for shadow-shops that specialize in that level of genetic modification. There aren't many, and we have to approach them quietly enough, politely enough, so that we don't burn bridges later with any of them that aren't hiding our prey. Second question. Do we think they went to ground on *Hurquar*?"

"It is an interesting parlor game," Marc replied. "They didn't want to bring him to *Zathus*, because that was our base and I have fingers everyplace they might have wanted to hide. They didn't stay long on *Orgoth Vortai*. Really just enough time to distract us and vanish. My guess is that their ultimate goal was *Hurquar* and no farther, at least until we find them, or the cops do. They'll need time to do whatever they have planned, so they needed to get ahead of us, but they have to stop running at some point so as to complete the work. After that, they can hide better. Yuudixtl and Vanir are two of the most common, least-insular species in the *Accord*. What do the authorities know?"

That last in a quieter voice as their waiter swooped by to refill water, replace bread, and pour more wine. This place really was top notch. Marc couldn't remember the last time he had eaten bread that good.

Possibly Gareth's mother's bread, at a winter break

celebration, but that would have been nearly eight years ago. He would have to come back to this town more.

"They got really quiet, there at the last on *Orgoth Vortai*," Maiair took up the thread. "We're facing Senior Constable Jackeith Grodray, one of Cinnra's worst enemies, and his new partner, Eveth Baker, another Vanir like Grodray."

"How good is Grodray?" Marc asked. "I've read Cinnra's notes, but he left out too much and self-aggrandized with the rest."

"He's good," Maiair replied. "Came close to unraveling us on a couple of occasions, back in the old days, when Cinnra first deposed Jeffrak and hadn't gotten rid of all the trouble-makers with axes to grind. Forced us to go much deeper underground than we ever had been before."

"Grodray's not the problem," Yooyar injected. "Baker is."

"How so?" Marc turned his attention to the youngest member of the gang, both in age and seniority. But the latter was just a matter of time, as he stared to recruit again. Then, she would suddenly be in the middle and need some responsibilities, to see if her natural talents could be honed down and polished into something like her sister.

"Grodray is methodical," Yooyar said. "Slow, careful, numbers-oriented. According to some of the old timers, he actually tracked us down with bank statements, wading through all the different transactions as we laundered things, spending a year just reading printouts. That's well and good. We learned to hide better. Baker is all action. She'll be the one that kicks in the door and stuns everyone in the room just so nobody gets away while she sorts out villains from innocent bystanders."

"Interesting," Marc observed. He turned to Zorge with a thin, cold smile. "When you nail down a probable target chop shop, let's feed the constables an anonymous tip. I want to see these two in action so I know what to prepare for. We know they're here. But they've gone to plainclothes work, so tracking them is harder. Let's flush everyone out at once."

"Understood," Zorge said.

Further conversation ceased as the food arrived. Marc considered the two pounds of rare steak in front of him, with all the fixings. He had rarely eaten this well back on Earth. At least not since he got drummed out of the Sky Patrol.

Maybe he needed to bring in a few more folks from the old neighborhood, once he was well and firmly in control around here. The *Accord of Souls* was an old lady walking home in a poorly-lit alley, just waiting to be mugged.

Maybe Marc needed to make himself king.

PLAINCLOTHES

IT FELT WRONG. Just wrong.

Eveth wasn't naked in public, but she sure felt that way, wearing civilian clothing as they chased down leads. Back home, she would still be in her bodysuit with the scale armor and the ring badge over her heart.

That intimidated people, however unconsciously. Vanir weren't the tallest species in the *Accord of Souls*, but they were the biggest, in terms of size and bulk. Eveth liked to use that to her advantage.

Here, she felt like an insurance salesman, cold-calling for new clients. Most of the people they had interviewed so far today had initially reacted that way when she and Grodray walked through the front door.

People got a lot less antagonistic when she dropped her wallet on the desk and flipped it open to reveal the badge inside, however

Still, they were making maddeningly-slow progress.

Slacks and a blazer did nothing to improve her humor.

Eveth checked the next address. Biomimetics Heavy Southern Industries LLKR.

The local Constabulary office had suggested that the place might be a cover for criminal activities. At no point, however had anybody ever been able to find anything even good enough to get a warrant that they could use as a wedge in the door, turn the place upside down with a fishing expedition.

She wondered if that just meant that the owners knew which local cops and politicians to bribe, to make sure that the authorities never knocked on their door.

She smiled to Grodray, checked the stun pistol tucked inside her jacket next to her insulating undershirt armor, and turned to her partner.

"Ready?"

"Let's go," he smiled sternly back.

Eveth stepped into the lift tube.

"Level Forty-seven," she said aloud.

What will those folks upstairs do when the Constables just show up out of the blue?

There couldn't be that many places left on *Hurquar* to hide. Three or four more stops, max, and they would have to rethink their approach. Maybe the human wasn't going to go out in public, and someone just had him on ice for now, until his violence could be unleashed.

In a way, that made her more comfortable. The thought of a human scaled up to Vanir-size was truly frightening. Most of the Accord were more of a size with humans, as she understood the file Jackeith had showed her. She could take a human in physical combat, unless he had been trained to mastery in one of the amazingly-common hand-to-hand fighting arts that all human cultures seemed to invent.

Did everyone on that planet study violence from the day they could walk?

The lift deposited her on the right floor without

providing any answers or solace. Grodray was there a moment later.

"Good cop?" she asked him as she strode down the unremarkable hallway towards a nice, wooden door at the end.

"Bad cop, Eve," he replied, telling her to take the lead. "The humans call it turning on the light in the middle of the night, to see what scurries for cover."

She nodded. Like her, he was getting tired of knocking on doors to bland faces and innocent shrugs. She could see that in his eyes. At least three of the places they had hit so far in the last two days had something about them that suggested to Eveth that a future police raid might be entertaining, but this case was too important to randomly kick over ant hills.

They needed to find a human on the loose, and do it without anybody who didn't already know finding out.

The office door was locked, so Eveth pressed the comm panel to the right side.

"Who is it?" a woman's voice answered a few moments later. A little light came on next to the speaker, indicating that the camera was working.

Eveth held up her badge, close enough to almost obscure any view of the hallway, and then lowered it so they could see how cross she had gotten today.

"Constabulary," she said simply. "We'd like to ask the principal researcher a few questions."

There. Nothing more. You don't need to know, if you're innocent. I don't need to spell it out, if you're guilty.

A fine game to play. A thin line to walk.

Long pause on the other end. Perhaps vermin scurrying? There was a team back at the precinct, watching for all auto-traffic in and out of this building right now. Anybody running would have the vehicle's controls remotely overridden and get them deposited nicely in a police parking lot for questioning.

And Eveth could run down anybody on foot.

That left only Elohynn, but there weren't that many in this city, and there were enough cameras available. They didn't prevent crime, because it was impossible to watch all the screens at once. Instead, they solved crime by letting investigators go back and track your every step afterwards.

The lock buzzed suddenly.

Eveth gave Grodray a shrug and opened the door. Inside was a corporate reception area so standard they might have all come out of the same decorating catalog. Desk where a receptionist would sit, currently empty. Polished wood walls with art. Two chairs and a sofa for people waiting for meetings.

This place varied from the basic design by including a *Brag Wall*. Eveth quickly scanned the images of a Nari woman: shaking hands with local politicians and others, accepting awards at various dinner ceremonies, and a couple of scholarly journal covers indicating a woman named Talyarkinash Liamssen published something really big inside.

Blue eyes. Fur just lighter than stone blue, with faint grayer stripes and black highlights. Eveth guessed her to be perhaps in her early thirties. Probably one of those brilliant researchers that finished all their degree work and realized that they would make more money opening a clinic catering to people trying to recapture lost youth, than trying to find gaps in the programs left by the Chaa or curing disease.

But there were always going to be people looking for immortality, however they could arrange it. Most of those folks would get scammed out of their money, but that wasn't Eveth's problem. It was the ones who might succeed that she had to handle.

Or folks willing to transform a human to hide him from the authorities.

Doctor Liamssen emerged from an inside door a moment later. The photos really didn't do the woman justice, or perhaps she had used her art on herself. Eveth would have said this woman was barely out of school rather than old enough to have established a corporation like this.

Eveth made a note to look her up later. Something just didn't smell right, already, and woman hadn't even spoken.

"Good afternoon," the Nari woman said carefully, pulling the door closed behind her so that three of them were alone in the front room. "I'm Doctor Liamssen. How may I help you, officers?"

"Constable Eveth Baker," she flashed the badge again, watching the woman's eyes for a reaction. "This is my partner, Senior Constable Grodray. We're investigating a smuggling case, and your organization came up in an offhand way. Normally, nothing, but the sensitivity of this case requires us to check off on every box individually, so we need to ask you some questions. Is there a conference room where we could talk?"

"I was actually in the middle of something…" the woman began.

"And we won't keep you very long, Dr. Liamssen," Eveth overrode her. "But we don't really have any flexibility here, and we'd like to get back to our case before the good leads grow cold."

Sharp blue eyes. Intelligent. Calculating the odds right now.

Everyone has something they want to hide. How hard did the good doctor want to push back on a pair of unknown Constables that just popped in for a bit of tea?

Eveth smiled. Dr. Liamssen smiled back, but it was plastic and brittle.

109

"Yes, I suppose," the doctor said. "If this won't take long."

"Just a few minutes, Dr. Liamssen," Grodray suddenly spoke up, his baritone voice drawing the woman's eyes and face back sharply.

The doctor was perhaps five foot eight, not counting her ears. A little taller than normal for a Nari female. Eveth was six foot seven, and out-weighed the woman by probably eighty pounds, all of it bone and muscle.

But Jackeith, the quiet one behind her, was seven foot one and three hundred pounds. Even as a skinny guy, the Nari would probably feel like a child next to a serious adult.

The look in the woman's eyes gave that much away.

She quickly led them back through the door into a large, spacious work area, with several black-topped workbenches that had seen hard use. Lighting overhead was bright and sharp, rather than friendly. Every blemish in anything would be shown.

Good thing to know about the occupant.

Eveth scanned the various things on workbenches, but couldn't even begin to describe them, let along classify things. Biomimetics, she seemed to remember, was about studying natural systems to replicate them in scaled-up formats, but how you did that wasn't something Eveth had ever bothered with.

At least this place wasn't breeding better food animals so she didn't have a wall of scared rabbits staring out at her, and all the fear/shit smell that went with it like that one time.

This place was almost a showroom, by comparison. Utterly clean ad lacking any personality.

The doctor led them to a small conference room off to one side, with a picture window looking back over the main room.

Eveth sat and pulled out her notebook to record a few thoughts.

"So what can I do for you, officers?" Liamssen said in a voice that was too forced to be calm and innocent.

But nobody was innocent.

"Smuggling," Eveth challenged the woman. "What do you know?"

It was a throwaway question. The sort of thing they taught you in police school to knock a subject off kilter. You didn't care what words came out of the suspect's mouth. Instead, you were watching how her mannerisms change when she's surprised.

When she forgets what lies she has prepared for them.

"Huh?" Liamssen replied, utter confusion resculpting her face, ears headed different directions, whiskers twitching a-harmonically.

"Sorry," Eveth wasn't, but it sounded good. "An organization that has dealt with you in the past has been accused of smuggling controlled chemicals without clearances or tax stamps. We need to eliminate you as fast as we can as a suspect. However, this is a very confidential case, so we can't tell you who they are. I was hoping we could take a quick scan of the premises and get a copy of your last ninety days' worth of inventory, just so we can mark you off the list and move on to the next place."

The eyes gave her away. She was good, but the nostrils flared a little too much, as if trying to smell the lies Eveth was peddling. The pupils expanded.

Eveth would have been willing to guess that the fur on the back of the Nari's scruff was standing up right now, hard as the woman was trying to hide it.

"I don't believe we keep those sorts of records on site," the doctor deflected well. "This is the lab, and most of the paperwork is in the main office. Is there something you can tell me? Perhaps I might be able to show you the right things?"

Eveth glanced significantly over a Grodray, as if asking permission. She was making it up as she went, and he knew that, but cops were never required to tell suspects the truth, except on the witness stand.

"Unlicensed genetic engineering," Eveth said in a conspiratorial tone, dropping her voice a little and adding a quaver of emotion.

She did it quite well today. Must be on.

"Oh?" the doctor countered, still off-balance.

"Someone is conducting experiments that go well beyond younger skin and different eyes, Doctor Liamssen," Eveth admitted on an awkward voice, watching the scientist's reaction. "Those require specialist chemicals that most labs have no need to maintain, so we just need to check your hazardous materials placards and refrigerator, and then we'll be on our way."

"Oh," the Nari brightened suddenly, like Eveth had just taken a weight off the woman's shoulders. She stood like an excited schoolgirl. "That we can do. Right this way."

Eveth smiled and rose, innocent as the dawn, and fell into the woman's wake. Out into the main room, so clean and well organized. Right to a four-ring binder thick with laminated cards and stamped with dates.

Eveth made it look like she was carefully checking things, flipping through them one at a time and making interested noises, plus occasional chuckles and harrumphs.

She had no idea what ninety percent of them even were, let alone what a geneticist might do with them. Didn't matter. She wasn't watching the notebook.

"The refrigerator?" Eveth asked after she had finished the notebook.

"There are two," the Nari doctor pointed across the room. "Or rather, the large one is at thirty-five degrees, and the small one is at fifteen below zero, depending on the materials we're working with in our experiments."

Eveth took the big one first. Inside, lots of vials and bottles for a pulse injector, plus a few larger bottles, none of which she could identify. Still, she pulled out her pocketcomm and dutifully took a couple of pictures so she had labels to inspect. The freezer differed only in that the bottles were usually metal, with screw-on lids and ice rimed on the outside. More pictures. More evidence, as it were.

"I think we've got everything we need, Doctor Liamssen," Eveth said brightly. She turned to her partner. "On to the next one?"

"Very good," he said. Grodray even bowed to the Nari woman. "Doctor Liamssen, thank you for your help."

"My pleasure," the woman said. "Will there be anything else?"

"No," Eveth said. "I've seen everything I need to. And we can show ourselves out. Thank you."

Grodray led. Eveth followed, twitchy because she didn't have her usual armor on, if a shot was going to strike her in the back she had turned.

But they made it to the door, unlocked it, and exited.

Jackeith didn't even look back, but walked right to the drop-tube.

"Ground floor," he said, vanishing.

Eveth was a step behind him, and a beat back at the first floor.

He stepped to a quiet corner and looked significantly.

"How soon can you get a warrant for that place?" she asked. "That woman's hiding something so big I thought her heart would explode."

"Agreed," he said. "I'll need twenty minutes or so to pass a message to the right people. They'll need another twenty to get us the paperwork we need. Think they'll wait that long up there?"

"Don't know," Eveth said. "I tried to play it casual, but she might have made us. You noticed how excited she was to show off the main room?"

"I did."

"I've never been in a working lab that clean," Eveth said. "Day one, something gets spilled, or set on fire, or broken. The only way that place is that clean…"

"Is if it has never been used, and what we saw was a stage for folks like us, if we broke in," he completed the thought. "We might have found our target. We've certainly found somebody. You wait here. I'll call this in and have all auto-traffic to the building locked down until we can land a Heavy Response Tactical Group on the roof."

Eveth moved to the front atrium of the building. A hex like this was impossible for one person to cover, but she found a tea shop table with a great view of the big, open space and settled herself in. Anyone emerging from the drop tube would be visible to her before they could slink out a side entrance.

And she could run down any human.

MADE

GARETH LOOKED up as Talyarkinash came down the secret stairs three at a time. He hadn't noticed before, because he was always studying her face for clues, but she was wearing shoes with no heel and barely any cushion, instead of the two to four inch heels most women, most *human* women, wore in public as a matter of course. And baggy, maroon pants that gathered at the ankle, vaguely like harem pants, plus a long, green tunic.

But the shoes were what threw him off. She wasn't human, so applying human fashion standards to the woman felt wrong. Off.

And human women wore skirts, not slacks. Right?

"We're made," she called out as she came into sight.

Gareth had found another room beyond the dentist chair and the music studio. There was a whole suite of rooms through there, as a matter of fact, but he was in a common room right now, seated on one end of a couch reading about the history of the *Accord of Souls* on a space tablet Talyarkinash had gotten for him.

Morty was on a barstool that telescoped down for a

Yuudixtl and up to a Nari-height bar. Xiomber was at a low table, eating a sandwich he had made from ingredients in a refrigerator in the kitchen, down the north hall.

Gareth had slept in a room down the south hall. At first, he had been concerned that the woman might try to slip into his room, in spite of his commitment to Pippa. He had locked the door just in case. But after that first afternoon, if she was going to do that, Gareth was pretty sure she'd be bringing a gun.

"What do you mean, made?" Morty asked. "We watched you on the screen. You did great."

"I don't know how, but that cop saw through everything," Talyarkinash said. "There should have been far more questions. Intrusions. Inspections. Annoyances. The last time the city wanted to check something, I had people in here for three days."

"She gave up too easily," Gareth observed, calmly powering off the magical book and placing it on the end table. Something had not felt right, but he hadn't been able to put a finger on it until Talyarkinash said something.

"Yes," the woman said. "I don't know why."

"She already knows you're guilty," Gareth said. "She left so that she could call for reinforcements to seal off the building without you being aware that the trap was closing."

"How would you know that?" Xiomber asked and then stuffed the last two bites into his mouth at once.

"That is how I would do it," Gareth said. "And I'm a cop. We need to run. Right now. If we're overreacting, we can come back tomorrow, but I doubt the building will still be an option in an hour. I've done this too many times to folks like you. I know what it feels like."

He rose and stretched. Action made him hungry, but there wasn't time to make a sandwich, and instinct told him their freedom might be measured in minutes.

"*Fardel*," Morty suddenly yelled, punching his pocketcomm. "We're screwed."

"What just happened? " Xiomber mumbled around his chewing.

"Two things," Morty snarled, lowering his chair and leaving the pocketcomm behind on the bar. "One, I tried to call a taxi, and the map somehow shows no available vehicles anywhere, in the middle of the afternoon. Two, the credit account I had been charging everything to suddenly locked up and shut itself down."

"Oh, crap," Xiomber rose.

"Yup," Morty agreed. "Normally, losing a credit account is nothing. We go through them all the time. Timing is exceptionally bad right now. Rather suspicious."

Gareth turned to see Talyarkinash pulling a duffel bag from a previously-closed cabinet.

Good idea. Gareth raced to his bedroom and grabbed his own bag. Everything had been cleaned and folded, ready to go.

Or run, as the case apparently was.

Amazingly, both of the brothers had also already grabbed bags, a soft sided satchel case for Morty, and backpack for Xiomber.

"What's the plan?" he asked.

Three days with these folks, and he had not really spent a lot of time on possible escape routes.

At first, sitting in that damned dentist's chair three more times and getting his brain psionically drilled had left him fuzzy for hours afterwards. Then watching as Talyarkinash and the brothers sketched out designs for a suit he could wear. Except it wasn't a suit, exactly.

Gareth hadn't really come to terms with what they had come up with.

But they had started designing something.

And now the clock was about to expire.

Its midnight, Cinderella.

"Yuudixtl are pretty common on this planet," Morty said. "If we split into two teams, Xiomber and I should be able to blend into a crowd well enough. Vanir and Nari tend to congress, so you two won't raise that big of an issue together. Talyarkinash, I'm sorry that we blew your cover with this. Do you have a bolt hole we can make?"

Gareth watched the woman pass through the stages of death in a few, quick seconds, lingering on anger for perhaps a touch too long, before she reached acceptance. She gave the brothers an address and fixed Gareth with a hard scowl.

"You better be worth it," she said.

"If I don't stop Maximus, I'm not sure anybody else can," he replied calmly. "The only price you're risking is jail."

That got through the woman's hard façade. The ears flickered forward and her whiskers even relaxed.

"We should go first," Gareth continued, turning to Morty and Xiomber. "If the Constables don't know you two, they'll key on me and you might be able to escape in the confusion."

"Where are we without you, Gareth?" Xiomber asked.

"Go back and build a new machine, Xiomber," he replied calmly. "Any Field Agent of the Sky Patrol you kidnap will be on your side as soon as you explain the situation to them. Invoke my name when you do."

"You're nuts, kid," Morty said.

"I'm Earth Force Sky Patrol, Morty," Gareth said. "That means something."

"Let's go," Talyarkinash snapped peevishly, pulling open yet another hidden door and stepping into the hallway only a few steps from the drop-tube.

"Second floor," she called, rather than first, and dropped from sight.

Gareth was right behind her.

The second floor of the building was a mezzanine that ran all the way around the outside of the building like a balcony. It was apparently made of glass, or aluminum that was functionally transparent, because for a moment Gareth thought he was floating in the air.

Talyarkinash had slung her bag's strap over a shoulder and added a jacket in the same rich maroon as her pants. Gareth was wearing what he thought of as his cowboy outfit: black pants, plaid shirt, blue denim jacket, no hat. The bag holding his clothes was more of a soft suitcase, so he had it by the handle, an oversized, pine-green briefcase as he walked.

The beautiful scientist had paused long enough for Gareth to come up on her left. She held out a hand and grabbed his. Bright blue eyes with a hint of fear in them looked up at him.

"Pretend we're on a trip together," she said calmly as she started to walk. "Maybe a honeymoon on a new planet. Walk like I'm your girlfriend."

He stared to say something, but swallowed it when he saw the abject terror in her eyes.

Being arrested and thrown in jail forever still didn't frighten her anywhere near as much as being this close to a human.

What in the nine hells did people in the *Accord* learn about humanity? Sure, we could be a rough folk. And probably too violent, especially since all species in the *Accord* had an empathic bond to them, but we aren't that bad.

Are we?

But he was Earth Force Sky Patrol. If nothing else, he had a duty to uphold the highest standards of conduct.

Gareth smiled at her and set off at a normal pace. Her ear tips were about as tall as he was, and their legs were roughly the same length. Her hand was clammy in his, and he didn't hold too tight.

Two young lovers, just landed and walking to a hotel. He could do this. And not even blush all that hard, because his heart was still true to Pippa, no matter how beautiful or forward some of the women of this new galaxy were.

Like he would have expected at home, there was an escalator to the ground floor. Six of them, in fact, one at each corner of the building. She led him to the one farthest from the front of the tower.

The atrium wasn't completely empty. It was mid-afternoon, and there were people coming and going. Tourists standing around. Messengers delivering packages.

Cover.

They rode the escalator down in the immediate wake of a Warreth mother and three chicks just about of an age to start school, back on Earth. They were full of questions about everything and kept their mother distracted.

Rather than stare, Gareth leaned against the side of the escalator and looked around the interior of the building. The architecture was unlike anything back home, with soaring, curved ribs like a giant whale holding the building up, instead of the normal squat pillars a human designer would have used. Curved panes of glass all around the outside made the inside feel like an aquarium, with him a prized fish on display.

Or a piranha.

Something drew his eye to the northeast corner of the ground floor. A tea shop was doing a brisk business this afternoon, catching people at that point in the day when they needed a jolt to make it through the rest of the work and then get home safe.

Someone was seated at the closest table to the center,

sipping tea and amiably watching the crowds ebb and flow around her.

He had never seen her in person, only through a remote camera hidden up in Talyarkinash's lab, but he had no doubt that the figure was Constable Eveth Baker.

Even across more than one hundred yards of space, Gareth felt her eyes lock on to him.

Gareth turned to Talyarkinash and nodded back to indicate the Constable. His eyes turned deadly serious.

"Run."

GAZELLES

EVETH WAS WATCHING THE DROP-TUBE, but like a good cop, she made sure to track the rest of the space. Jackeith would be back with reinforcements in under an hour. All she had to do was bottle them up, nice and cozy on the forty-seventh floor in their cute, fake, lab.

Until she had that Nari liar handcuffed in an interrogation room, sweating, while a heavy-armed strike team cleared the space with live weapons.

Eveth was looking forward to that part. This had been a hard week.

She saw the Warreth and chicks descend from the mezzanine. Probably taking pictures of the river before heading home for dinner. Two other tourists followed, quietly enjoying their trip.

Something about the male caught her eye. Vanir male. Nari female. The light was bad at this distance, odd afternoon shadows distorting things, but something wasn't right. Something about the image of the male.

He wasn't anything special from this distance. Casually

dressed in a style she didn't recognize. Blond hair. Broad shoulders. A little short.

Short.

Nari females tended to run about five and a half feet tall. The Warreth woman in front of them looked about the same, so the man was a little over six feet tall. Short for a Vanir.

Tall for a human.

The man turned and made eye contact with her like he was seated across the table, rather than nearly one hundred twenty yards away.

Recognition, like an electric shock running through both of them, apparently.

He turned to say something to his companion, nudging her forward as the Warreth mother gathered up her brood and started across the tile plaza.

Eveth was already out of her chair and moving.

The human had the woman by the hand and was tugging her along now. She resisted at first, until she saw Eveth moving, and then those long, Nari legs started to churn.

Eveth didn't bother to yell. The distance was too great, and those two weren't about to listen to her.

And the last thing Eveth needed to do today was to start a panic about a human loose in Olehmmishqu.

Civilian clothes drove her almost to distraction as she picked up speed. In her bodysuit, there was a pouch on her right thigh, opposite her holster, for a pocketcomm. In mufti, she had been forced to stuff in into an interior breast pocket of the blazer.

The two fugitives had made it to the exterior door now. Hopefully, they would try to call for an auto-taxi, gambling that the vehicle would arrive before she did, except that Grodray's contacts had already set up a hard lock on all calls, two blocks in every direction.

She pushed harder, closing the space to the door as they turned right and began to move.

All the two fugitives would get was an angry cop closing as fast as her Vanir legs could carry her.

She was at the door, jammed it open with her immense mass moving at high speed, and took off after them.

Eveth was confident she could run down any human.

Still, she needed backup. And help cornering them.

She pulled out the pocketcomm and triggered a call to her partner.

It rang twice before he picked it up.

"Talk to me, Eve," he said urgently.

"I've got two runners, Grodray," she said.

Any other words were lost as she plowed squarely into a pedestrian coming around a corner from the alley, one of the Tree People, built about as sturdy as an oak.

All the breath whooshed out of her and Eveth felt her skull crack hard on the man's trunk. Fortunately, she had a really hard head.

But her pocketcomm slid away, still moving when she stopped.

The Tree Person looked down at her in surprise and offered a hand up, along with an apology.

Eveth took it, but couldn't see her pocketcomm through the wobbly stars dancing circles around her head. Down at the far end of the block, the human and his accomplice had already crossed a street and were threatening to melt into the afternoon rush hour mobs that were just starting to emerge from buildings.

She had a choice, but it was never really in doubt.

Eveth could always track down her pocketcomm later. It would lock up in ten seconds, and Grodray could send a pulse to make it scream fit to wake the dead, once he realized she had lost it.

But in the meantime, the human would vanish into the underworld, and Eveth was pretty sure they would never get another chance like this to capture him. He had a top geneticist helping him to escape. In three days, he might look like anything at all.

Eveth growled out her rage and began to run. Since she couldn't call for backup, she would just have to do this on her own.

She reached inside the jacket and pulled out her stun pistol. The range was too great now, but that was just a matter of anger and patience.

Right up her alley.

HUNTED

GARETH COULD HAVE EASILY outrun Constable Baker on a track. One of the horror elements of the species descriptions in the book he had been reading spelled out the immense endurance and stamina of humans compared to every other species in known space, including the presumably-horrifying little fact that some human societies had been known to chase their pray to death, jogging lightly along for hours until the creature simply collapsed of exhaustion and died.

Only Terran dogs, Humanity's secret weapon, could match humans for endurance.

He would have liked to tell the writers of such lurid squamph that the average human worked in a factory or at a desk, and was about as dangerous as the average citizen here, but they wouldn't listen. He was a human, after all.

And it wasn't Gareth against a single Constable. He had Talyarkinash to protect, and a strange and wondrous city into which he could easily become so disoriented that he became an easy target for some innocent beat cop.

Gareth would not kill an authorized law enforcement

agent doing their job. He wouldn't even hurt one any more than necessary to escape.

He had to represent all humans to the *Accord of Souls*. On his life would be their eventual welcome into broader galactic society.

Fortunately, rush hour was apparently the same, the galaxy over. Happy hour had dawned and people were starting to sneak out of offices a little early to get a head start on family life, or extra time down at the corner bar.

Just in the few seconds since they had emerged from the building and gone a block, the number of people on the sidewalk had practically doubled. Gareth was hard pressed not to run into people hard enough to knock them down, especially while also not losing Talyarkinash's hand.

She was his lifeline right now, and he needed her like a lifesuit in a hull breach. Fortunately, she needed him just as much. Without Gareth and the brothers, she would have nowhere to go when the police did come back and started going through her files.

He tried not to shout out his internal joy that another criminal ring would be broken, because that meant he was about to go down with them. A cop like Eveth Baker would shoot first and he would wake up behind bars for the rest of his life, while they tried to figure out a way to completely wipe his memory without taking the rest of his mind with it.

That woman had the look about her.

And she was chasing them, gun in hand and down by her side like a well-trained operative. Gareth understood instinctively how dangerous she would be.

At the corner, the light held them for a second. Gareth glanced back and picked her up through the mass of bodies as she came after them. He watched Baker run into a walking tree (*A **WALKING TREE**?*) and lose her communications device, the handheld sliding under a car parked at the curb.

It gave him an idea as the light turned to walk.

"Talyarkinash, I need you to trust me," he said as they pressed their way forward through the growing mob of strangely-smelling folks.

He felt her dig her heels in hard, because she stopped moving and he nearly pulled her over accidentally.

"Trust you?" she snarled quietly. "You?"

"I think I can get us away from her, but I need your help," Gareth said. "Your trust. I swear that I will do everything I can to protect you, on my honor as a Field Agent of the Earth Force Sky Patrol."

"Are you insane, Gareth?" she hissed.

Gareth decided that they were losing ground to Constable Baker while arguing. He pulled the Nari scientist along by sheer strength.

"Maybe," he admitted as she allowed herself to fall into stride again.

It was like pushing against ocean waves to get to the calmer, open water, getting through the press of bodies.

There. An alley way between two buildings, possibly allowing industrial vehicles access to interior loading bays. The asphalt was worn and dirty, and no plants lined the walls.

He looked back and Baker had chosen pursuit over assistance. She was holding her gun and had foregone her radio for backup.

Gareth pulled Talyarkinash into the alleyway, like two young lovers sneaking off for a quick smooch out of the flow of traffic. Nothing could be further from his mind, but anything to confuse people worked in his favor.

Like New Metropolis back home, the streets were movie set facades, pretty on the street, but unwashed, ugly, and industrial in the alleys. Gareth counted dumpsters, trashcans, a parked delivery truck, and several overhead balconies, possibly good, old-fashioned fire steel escapes. None of the latter provided him the cover he needed, but the rest of the space would do.

Gareth measured off the strides he needed, pulling Talyarkinash along with him.

"She'll be here in seconds," he said urgently. "I need you stretched out on the asphalt here, like you've tripped and twisted your ankle, and I didn't stop. She'll see you, and come to arrest you. I'm hiding close by. I will jump her when she gets here. Can you do that?"

"The alternative is jail?" Talyarkinash asked.

"The alternative is Maximus finds out you've been helping me and the brothers, and kills you," Gareth said simply. "I'm trying to prevent that right now. Later, I need your help to save the galaxy."

The terror was still there in those ocean-deep eyes, like icebergs floating on a storm-tossed, angry sea. But something else appeared.

He might have been bold enough to call it hope, if he wanted to push his luck.

"You'll protect me?" she asked quietly.

"I promise," Gareth stated.

Before he could react, she lunged forward and kissed him, one arm around his neck and whiskers tickling his face. She felt ice-cold initially, but warmed in the second he held her.

"Go," she ordered, tossing her bag further down the alley and stretching herself out, just as he had explained it.

Gareth loped over to one of the dumpsters and crawled into a shadow cast by the delivery truck, face all a-blush. Now all he had to do was hope that the driver was too busy having a smoke to come out in the next thirty seconds.

"Come back here, you bastard," Talyarkinash suddenly yelled at the top of her lungs. "You can't leave me."

Gareth nearly surged out of his hiding place, then stopped himself. He peeked anyway.

Talyarkinash honestly looked like she was watching him run away from where she had fallen, as a cowardly Gareth had panicked and fled.

Like he had done the absolutely unthinkable and left one of his own behind.

But humans had no reputation for honor here, either.

"Gareth," Talyarkinash yelled. "Come back."

"Freeze," an angry woman called.

Gareth recognized the voice from the building.

Constable Baker, right on time. Hopefully alone.

Talyarkinash stopped yelling. Glanced back and moaned wretchedly.

"Oh, you bastards," she cried. "All of you."

"Where is he?" Baker yelled.

From the volume, she had entered the mouth of the alley. Probably in a two-handed stance, one hand cupped under the other to steady her pistol, since she didn't have the walkie-talkie with her. Most likely turned thinways to her target to reduce her silhouette.

Gareth held his breath.

"Where is he?" Baker repeated.

"Bastard abandoned me," Talyarkinash replied angrily. "I fell down and couldn't get up, so he just ran."

"Show me your hands," Baker ordered.

Gareth couldn't see the Constable when he slid an eye even with the edge of the dumpster, but Talyarkinash was in clear sight, ignoring him as she faked a bum leg and held her hands up.

"Roll over on your stomach, hands behind your back," Baker called.

She had to be walking slowly closer, as the echoes

softened. Gareth might have done the same thing, approaching carefully and by the book.

Knowing who he was dealing with, Gareth might also have just shot the criminal on the ground with the stunner, to be sure. Talyarkinash had a dangerous edge underneath that scholarly brain.

But the Nari woman complied. Laid out flat with her hands behind her.

Trusting Gareth to save her life.

The surge of pride made him feel ten feet tall.

Shadows on the pavement as Baker got close. Gareth could track her now, with enough sun behind her.

He would be reaching for handcuffs about now. Moving towards his weak hand side so he could hold the pistol while snapping a cuff over a wrist.

Baker was left-handed, she would be shifting towards him, and turning her back on his hiding place.

He hoped.

There.

Now or never.

Gareth rose on silent feet and exploded out of his hiding place.

He had to pretend Baker wasn't a girl as he was about to tackle her. All of his soul cried out in shame at hitting a woman, and doing it from behind as well.

Her being half a head taller, and almost as broad in the shoulders helped. He was back on the muddy turf, bringing down a burly tight-end short of the goal line to save the play, the game, and the season.

Slamming into her felt like that tackle had been. Damn, she must outweigh him, too.

The woman must have had a sixth sense. Something warned her and she glanced back at the last instant, tangled up with gun, cuffs, prisoner, and rampaging human.

They ended up in a jumble of bodies, but Gareth used all his training to force his way on top. She was muscled like a tight-end as well, so he didn't have time to wrestle with her. Not if he wanted to survive.

God only knows what kinds of martial arts *Accord* cops were taught.

Instead, he broke every rule his mother had hammered into him as a child. He had hit a girl. Knocked her down and pinned her to ground.

Gareth punched her in the middle of the forehead, as hard as he could. It was like trying to open a coconut with a fist.

But it worked. Her head bounced off the hard pavement almost as hard as it had his fist and her eyes lost focus.

He punched her a second time, wailing inside at the thought of his father finding out when he came home. Another bounce.

This time she stayed down.

He checked her eyes. They were half rolled back, unfocused, but symmetric, so he had just knocked her out cold and into a mild concussion.

Still, he climbed up and rolled her onto her side so she wouldn't somehow choke. The handcuffs had fallen just about with them, which was fortuitous.

Gareth grabbed Agent Baker and lifted her enough to shift her over to the dumpster he had used as cover. A quick snap and the handcuffs latched her to a ton of steel. He had no idea what a key might look like, but hopefully this would be enough of a peace offering.

He was a human. He was supposed to be a mindless, killing machine threatening all civilization with bloodshed.

Maybe, just maybe he could communicate with them by *not* using violence.

"Not bad, buddy," another voice said. High tenor, nasty tones.

Gareth looked up at a Warreth male, standing in the mouth of the alley, holding a gun on him.

This one didn't look like a cop. Too slovenly, compared to Agent Baker and her partner.

Gareth was willing to gamble that he had just found one of Sarzynski's men.

"Stand up slowly, human," the birdman said, confirming the first estimation.

Only one of Maximus's men would know him by species on sight.

Gareth complied, hands out but not overhead. His mind was racing with options, but the birdman was far enough away that he could probably shoot Gareth without a problem.

He needed to get out of this alley, and quickly.

And he really needed to be away from all of this before somebody's backup arrived.

"You work for Maximus?" Gareth asked carefully.

"That's right," the Warreth gunman said with a sneer. "Told us to watch the cops. Follow them around, in case they led us to you. And lookie what we have here."

"I'd rather not," Talyarkinash said.

She shot the man with Baker's gun, both of them forgotten in all this excitement.

Gareth realized just how lucky he could be.

"Thank you," Gareth told her as she emerged from behind the delivery truck, pistol in hand pointed at the thug.

"I did owe you one," she smiled up at him. "What do we do with them?"

"Is that a stunner?" he asked.

"Yes," she said. "Hers."

"Can you adjust the stun?"

"Sure."

"Put it on the highest setting and shoot him again," Gareth said. "How long will he be out?"

"Probably hours," she replied, adjusting something with her other hand and then shooting the birdman again. "Now what?"

"Now I would like you to put the gun back in Agent Baker's holster," Gareth said. "And then we're going to run like hell."

"You just knocked her out," Talyarkinash said. "She'll be awake long before he is."

"And she'll have her handcuffs, badge, and gun," Gareth agreed. "I'm trying to send them a message."

"What message?"

"That we're on the same side," Gareth said.

RESCUED

"I DON'T CARE," Eveth growled, holding an icepack to her face and forehead. "He's mocking us."

"And he could have killed you, Baker," Grodray replied mildly.

It didn't help that her partner was probably right. She had come to, handcuffed to the dumpster with her own manacles. Badge and gun were tucked into their spots. Unconscious thug with a rap sheet a mile long stunned and laid out at her feet.

She had just managed to free herself when Grodray arrived with half a dozen uniforms holding weapons out.

Now, they were all back up on the forty-seventh floor, taking Talyarkinash Liamssen's life apart. No reason to waste a perfectly good warrant. And she had found an icepack in a personal refrigerator, down a set of steps concealed by a bookcase and hiding a medium-sized apartment.

Grodray had taken charge of things at that point, setting her down in that sterile conference room upstairs with instructions not to move while forensics teams went to work.

"What do we know?" Eveth asked, raging inside but controlling it.

She couldn't believe she had fallen for something so obvious. The human was dangerous, that much she knew. Half a foot shorter, but roughly the same mass, and extremely strong. And he had a punch like a wallop. Her head was still ringing.

"The two Yuudixtl were probably here with them," Grodray said, reading off his notes. "We've found indications four people were staying downstairs, and at least one was the right size. They had been here three days, from the trash in the can and the food missing."

"Missing?" Eveth asked, still a little fuzzy.

"Count slices of bread missing from a loaf, divide by two, and you have meals served," Grodray smiled. "Things like that. Crude but effective."

"Right."

"The Yuudixtl obviously disappeared when you went after the others, and we have no witnesses," Grodray continued. "Cameras probably caught something, but it will take time to track that down. I'm sure they made it outside the lock-down zone and called a cab with a new credit account they had stolen."

"Sirs, you might want to see this," one of the cops, a young Grace officer with good instincts, had appeared in the door and motioned them to join in.

"What have you got?" Grodray was first, only because Eveth had to stand up, wobble the tiniest amount, and then follow.

"Not sure," the male cop said. "We think she was in a hurry to destroy things, but missed this."

They followed him out into the main room, down the stairs, and into a small work area off the main control room with the worthless music studio deck. Liamssen had done something to the computer controlling it all, and none of the knobs or sliders did anything now, as far as anybody could tell.

Another officer was standing there, holding a piece of paper that had been crumpled up at some point, now flattened out on the desktop.

Eveth leaned over the Grace cop's shoulder to look. The tentacles were almost painful on her head and neck, but she could deal with that. Except that everywhere those tentacles touched, the pain receded.

She glanced down at the officer in surprise. He smiled sheepishly and blushed.

"Thought it might help," he offered.

"It does," Eveth replied. "Thank you."

He leaned closer. She leaned closer. It was almost like they were kissing, except both were faced to the side. It was still a bizarre experience, one that should have been erotic, under almost any other circumstances.

The paper was a sketch, drawn freehand but by an extremely skilled hand. It showed a wing, such as an Elohynn might have, coming out from the back and down to a central elbow joint, before running up to a rough point overhead.

But the scale was all wrong, if the lengths on the side were any indication.

An Elohynn male, roughly six feet tall on average, had wings that were roughly nine feet long, with a twenty-foot wingspan on a mature adult.

This wing would be almost three times that.

"Any ideas?" Grodray asked.

Eveth pulled clear of the forest of helpful kelp and stood fully upright with a nod of thanks to the cop.

Grodray was deduction writ large. Eveth had always suspected the reason she was paired with him, once the bosses realized that they wouldn't hate each other, was that she brought induction to the equation.

Leaps of intuition that the evidence just wouldn't cover.

"Ornithopter?" she tossed out.

It was utterly inefficient, since something like an auto-car rode powered lifters and could also maneuver in low planetary orbit once a transport tube had lifted you. But the Elohynn preferred personal flying to anything else, including walking.

But why would a human want to build an Ornithopter?

She shrugged after a moment.

"Where did you find this?" Grodray pointed at the page.

"Crumpled up and behind the waste drop, sir," the Grace cop said. "Looks like someone didn't like the design, but missed the incinerator bucket, and were either too lazy to get up, or didn't see it fall long."

"Tag it and scan it into the files," Grodray instructed the man.

Eveth followed her partner into the main common room where obviously the criminals had been waiting. There were remains of a sandwich on a low table, a pocketcomm that one of the Yuudixtl had been using to access a stole credit account on the bar, and a reading tablet on the end table next to the sofa.

"Three of them in here, watching us upstairs?" Eveth asked, taking it all in at a glance.

"That's my theory, Eve," Grodray said. "Given the timelines, Liamssen came down stairs as soon as we left, everyone panics. They run, taking the time to grab go-bags from that cabinet over there, and to tell the computers to kill themselves."

"So we've found them, and lost them," Eveth said. "Now what?"

"Now we turn up the heat," Grodray smiled with a cruel

mouth and lips pressed thin. "Assault on a Constable. Flight From Justice. And we have Dr. Liamssen's full bio signature, plus a good description of the other three."

"Do we lock the city down?" Eveth asked.

"Had you been hurt, or killed, I would have gotten nasty, Eve," Grodray said in a voice that managed to make even a hardened cop like Eveth shiver. "The perp did the absolute minimum necessary to escape you, plus he left us a prize, like a cat bringing home a mouse. I want to sweat that Warreth hard and open up a second avenue of the investigation, but we're going to hand the punk off to another team so we can focus on the perp."

"Can you do that?" she asked, suddenly breathless with anticipation. This was up there with Level-7 Security.

"I talked to the Planetary Inspector while the medics were checking you out," Grodray stated. "She's cleared us to act like free agents here."

Free agents. Just a tiny step short of Prime Inspector, the dream of every cop, to be able to pursue any crime they thought warranted their attention, on any planet of the *Accord of Souls*, and demand the full cooperation of the local authorities.

Not request. Demand.

Jackeith Grodray had said he never wanted to get to that level. Hell, he had never gone farther than Senior Constable, but that was a personal choice that Eveth would never settle for.

But Grodray had a Level-7 Security Authorization. Had they offered him Prime Inspector at some point and he refused?

Eveth made a note to learn as much as she possibly could from the man while they were partnered. Jackeith Grodray had always been exceptional, spoken of in the department in reverential tones. Was he even better than that?

"Step one?" Eveth asked after she got her thoughts under control.

"Dinner," Grodray said. "I know a good take-out joint not far from here, so we can move quickly if we get a hit on an All-Points Bulletin in the next hour. Then I'm going to turn up the heat and see what boils."

Again, Eveth felt a shiver at the tone. She wasn't sure she had ever seen Grodray lose his temper, but that was what this felt like.

Which was good, because she was well past that point with the damnable human running loose in her city.

ESCAPED

MORTY BREATHED a sigh of relief as the *maître d'* settled them in a semi-private room just outside the kitchen and left menus.

"Shouldn't we be making our way to Talyarkinash's backup place?" Xiomber asked soberly before taking a long drink of water.

"Yes and no," Morty replied, studying his brother for signs of wear or fear. "The lab's been burned now. And we know the other two got away, or the cops would have made a much bigger stink about catching a human. Somebody would have leaked that to a news crew, regardless of the situation."

"Okay, so we all got away," Xiomber agreed. "And?"

"So now we have a secondary duty to look after ourselves, egg-brother," Morty said. "Like Gareth said, if he gets taken, it will be up to us to build a new generator array and kidnap another cop from Earth, if we want to stop Maximus. We can't do that from inside a jail cell."

"You think Talyarkinash's other place will get raided?" Xiomber asked.

"I don't know," Morty admitted. "But we're hiding from the cops, the Constables, and Maximus now. That doesn't leave us a lot of places to go, because Talyarkinash would have needed underworld help to set up her bolthole in the first place. Somebody knows. The question is how quickly they'll talk, and that hinges on either fear of Maximus or a good enough reward from the cops."

Xiomber followed Morty's logic as he emptied his water glass. It had been a nerve-wracking couple of hours. He was a scientist, not a bank robber. A good salad and a pasta right now would help calm him, because they needed to find a way to set up their own bolthole on this planet. One where they could hide from agents of Maximus and the law at the same time.

"How long can we run?" Xiomber asked, calming enough to go through the implications.

"We spent a month setting this gig up," Morty reminded the man. "Once we realized that Maximus wasn't going to just settle for being the kingpin of the criminal underground but wanted to rule everything. It was only a matter of time before he brought in more humans to help. I've got eight more credit accounts we can access right now, and connections to a couple of brokers for more, so we're good for money. I know a few places we might could hide, but it depends on the Constabulary now. I'm expecting random, armed raids on a number of them tonight, expressly looking for any of four known fugitives. We cleaned up Talyarkinash's lab well enough, but we were in a hurry and the cops will find enough."

"So hiding in plain sight at a restaurant is a good idea?" Xiomber rolled his eyes.

"Cops aren't going to roust this place," Morty replied. "And there are probably thirty other Yuudixtl in here right now, so we don't stand out. This buys us another couple of hours, then I know an all-night tea house in a nice part of town, over by the university. We can hang out there, as long as you don't mind open mic poetry night."

Xiomber rolled his eyes again, but Morty expected that. His egg-brother was not a bohemian by any stretch of the word. But cops would never look in a tea house filled with weird kids playing guitars and chanting bizarre performance art to total strangers.

In the morning, if they were still able and the idea still sounded good, they could make their careful way to where Talyarkinash was hopefully hiding with Gareth, and move on to the next step. Or just run and find themselves another place to hide while they worked on a different plan to save the universe.

Damn the Constables for being good enough, smart enough, or maybe lucky enough to have broken things so wide open, so early. Morty had been counting on having at least a another week, and then it would have been someone from the old gang sniffing around.

Talyarkinash could have deflected them long enough, and then Morty and his brother could have unleashed an avenging angel on people who seemed to want to take the whole damned *Accord of Souls* down.

Didn't those fools understand that you had to have a working society first?

Morty could see a dark future where Maximus got himself made over into an emperor. He would have to institute a reign of brutality to keep power, which would mean more humans, until all of the old species of the *Accord*, bound by their psionic empathy, became a permanent slave class to a caste of humans and other murderous criminals.

If Morty had realized all this a year ago, when Cinnra

decided he needed a personal killer to keep power, Morty might have quit and turned state's evidence then. Better jail than the sort of dystopian future Morty might have personally helped give birth to.

He could only hope that it truly was possible to fight fire with fire.

At least he and his egg-brother had managed to destroy the wormhole station back on *Zathus*. Maximus wouldn't be able to bring in more humans until he built a new one, and that would take time, especially if the cops were watching, and the overlord had lost his two best physicists to crises of conscience.

The waiter came and took their orders. Morty had wanted some wine, just to help with his nerves, but Xiomber overrode him. And he would let his brother do that. It was only fair, if he was going to drag Xiomber to a poetry slam later.

"I hate you, by the way," Xiomber mentioned as the waiter left.

"What did I do this time?" Morty asked.

"You're going to turn me into one of the good guys, you bastard," his brother snapped. "All our lives we've wanted to be criminals, you know. Could have gotten legitimate jobs, but that was too staid. And now I'm running for my life from every goomba and cop in this town."

"Sorry," Morty offered.

"Is it ever going to get better, you suppose?" Xiomber asked.

Morty shrugged.

"We have to save galactic civilization from a madman first," Morty replied. "And then deal with a human cop that we've turned into a god, and a criminal underworld that won't forgive us, either way. I'm happy enough to be in the frying pan right now, because the alternative is the fire itself."

"Do we turn ourselves in?" Xiomber asked. "Tell the cops everything, including what we plan for Gareth, and see if they can stop Maximus?"

"They won't believe us," Morty said. "We've already shredded the law books at this point. *Fardel* only knows how many centuries we'd be sentenced too, even with time off for good behavior. Gareth would be in the cell with us, or a zoo, which is the same thing. Maximus would dance right around any traps they thought they could set to catch him, and then end up grand poohbah of everything."

"No," Xiomber countered. "I mean *everything* we know. The crooked cops. The suborned prosecutors. The Constables Maximus secretly recruited. Everything."

"We wouldn't live to see the inside of a jail cell, brother," Morty replied mournfully.

"It might be worth trying," Xiomber said.

"We'll give Gareth a shot first," Morty said. "I think he has what it takes to do this."

"And if he succeeds, brother?" Xiomber snapped. "We're still guilty of breaking just about every law on the books. You think they'll just kiss us on the snout and send us on our way?"

"I think that I would enjoy spending the rest of my life in the next cell over from Maximus," Morty retorted. "At least the rest of the *Accord of Souls* would have survived, at that point. That's way better than some of the options I can see right now."

Xiomber wanted to say something sarcastic and biting to that. Morty could see it in his eyes, almost taste it in the scent his egg-brother gave off. But Xiomber held his silence.

Morty knew why.

He was right.

In the end, if the *Accord* didn't survive, being outside the jail wouldn't mean much of anything.

Because Morty had been the one who had done the most to tear it down.

SAFE

GARETH OPENED THE DOOR FIRST, Talyarkinash standing off to one side in case somebody was waiting inside and opened fire. Not that there was much of anything he could do if the game was indeed up, but it made him feel better.

In addition to a couple of bags of takeout food they had grabbed a few blocks over, she still had the pistol she had taken off the thug, to replace Constable Baker's sidearm. That punk wouldn't be needing it again. It was in her hand now, only shaking a little bit as the toils of the day took their toll on the Nari woman.

Talyarkinash wasn't nearly as fragile as the human women he had known. Most of them, anyway. Pippa might have had a heart of gold, but there was still a spine of titanium. She and Talyarkinash might have seen eye to eye on many things, although they would never meet.

Thinking about his beloved helped him frame the Lynxwoman scientist better. Women in the *Accord* weren't soft creatures that needed to be protected at all costs. That cop had almost been tough enough to take him singlehandedly, after all.

And Talyarkinash hadn't shrunk from shooting the Warreth in the alley to save his life.

Gareth took a deep, confused breath, and pushed the door open. It was made of some light but extremely durable plastic and swung inward on silent hinges.

Inside, he found a traditional flat, with a compact kitchen and dining area on his right, and a long, skinny salon on the left. The furniture in here was odd, but Gareth put that down to Talyarkinash's personal tastes.

The couch was an open, wooden frame with a single pad that folded in the middle, rather than the sort of thing he had known growing up, overstuffed and upholstered, with lace doilies on the back.

A chair in the front corner appeared to be a square, metal-tube frame with a kickstand back. A single piece of black canvas had been sewn around the frame in such a way as to form a person-sized hammock, for lack of a better way to describe it.

Instead of a big wooden armoire to hold the entertainment system, there was a single flat panel thinner than his thumb, maybe a yard across, hung from the wall across from the couch-thing, with odd-looking shelves below it. Each shelf appeared to be a wooden box about eighteen inches deep and eighteen or thirty-six inches wide. They were stacked up and leaned against the wall, providing a variety of flat spaces to put books and other knick-knacks.

Down the left side of the center wall, Gareth could see a door he presumed was a restroom, and another to her bedroom.

Nobody was visible when Gareth entered the room. He quickly confirmed the other two spaces were what he thought, and empty, returning to find Talyarkinash standing in the salon, arms wrapped around herself and shivering.

Gareth wanted to walk up and wrap his own arms around the woman to help comfort her, but that didn't sound like a good idea. It might remind her she was supposed to be afraid of him.

Instead, he moved to the counter where she had set the food and began unpacking things onto the table. Protein and calories would be a good idea right now, as he had missed dinner while they slunk through back alleys and quiet streets, making sure they didn't have a tail of any kind.

"Food?" he asked, trying to break through the wall of frost that had seemed to settle itself around the scientist.

She visibly shuddered once, drawing a deep breath, but she joined him, pulling two bowls from a cabinet and filling glasses with water.

They sat at a low table that reminded Gareth of ancient Japan. Pillows on the floor in various colors instead of chairs, so he kicked off his shoes and knelt. The table itself appeared to be a two foot by four foot sheet of three-quarter inch plywood, painted black and enameled over. Looking underneath, it was held up by an overturned, red milk carton.

Weird.

Gareth presumed it was an artistic statement of interior decorating, rather than poverty. Maybe a cover as a poor student, since this was where she went to hide, expecting the police to be waiting at her regular apartment.

She joined him, digging into the food with chopsticks. He had never learned the trick to eating with two sticks, so Gareth had to settle for an odd, plastic device that combined a spoon with short tines from a fork.

"Do we know when Morty and Xiomber will arrive?" he

asked after selecting a random mix of colors and shapes into his bowl.

She shrugged and chewed. After a moment, she took a drink and fixed him with a focused gaze.

This was when a medusa would turn him to stone. Fortunately, his associate tonight was a Nari, and not a Grace.

Gareth surprised himself by not freaking completely out to be surrounded by aliens of all shapes, sizes, and colors. Pastor Jacob would probably expect that they were all going to hell, but they really were good people, the ones he had met so far.

"We can't even be sure *that* they will join us," she said in a cold, hard voice. "If we get caught, you told them they had to build a new machine and get another human agent to help. They might have gone off to do that as an insurance policy."

"Oh," Gareth commented neutrally. "I had not considered that."

"And I think we should move quickly ourselves, regardless of when we see them," Talyarkinash continued. "I have all my notes, even if I had to destroy everything at the lab. And it will be extremely experimental, beyond anything I've ever tried before, and dangerous, but I'm not sure what I can do to mitigate that, so we don't gain much time by waiting."

"You were ready when the Constables showed up?" Gareth asked. Nobody had told him that.

"Close enough," she admitted. "The next step was to mix reagents and test them against human DNA, and I can do that first thing tomorrow."

"You have a lab here?"

He was shocked. Just in case, Gareth had examined every room, but detected no sign.

"The back of the linen closet has a hidden door," she said. "I own the next flat over on this floor and I converted it into a small lab, just for this exact circumstance, the need to do something when I couldn't work downtown."

"Wow," Gareth managed.

For a Field Agent of Earth Force Sky Patrol, he was certainly getting a first-class education in the criminal mind this week. The bad guys back home were never going to escape him. If he ever found a way to return.

Dinner went quickly. Gareth watched her put a few containers in the refrigerator and the rest into an incinerator slot on the wall. He moved to the weird-looking sofa and decided it was wide enough. He grabbed a blanket from the linen closet in the bathroom while she watched and took off his boots.

"What are you doing?" she asked.

"Going to sleep," Gareth replied. "I'm tired and tomorrow already feels like a busy day."

"But on the couch?" Talyarkinash pressed.

Gareth fixed her with his own, serious gaze.

"Yes," he said firmly.

As a contest of wills, it was over quickly.

Gareth thought he detected a sag in her otherwise-rigid spine, and then she walked past him.

"Okay," she said mildly. "Good night."

"Good night," he replied, stretching himself out as much as he could.

When his weight shifted, Gareth discovered that the back and bottom moved on sliders built into the sides. He got up, tugged experimentally on the bottom, and was rewarded when the entire thing slid out and flat, providing him a bunk wider than he had back at the Arsenal, and long enough, if he slept diagonally, to stretch out.

Lovely invention.

He got horizontal and started to relax.

Up the hallway, the light under Talyarkinash's door went out after a few minutes and the apartment fell into silent darkness.

Gareth knew he should be sleeping. However, the day had been too much for him to unwind quickly, so he listened to the building creak. The walls themselves were thick enough to obscure the sounds of neighbors, but fans blew warm air about, and the refrigerator hummed to itself occasionally, keeping his mind too alert.

After fifteen minutes or so, Gareth heard the bedroom door open, and bare feet pad quietly across the carpet. His eyes had adjusted to the dimness, so he could see Talyarkinash, dressed in a pair of long, silken pajamas, walk into the center of the room.

Rather than speak, Gareth waited, unsure what was going through the beautiful alien's mind. At least she wasn't holding a gun.

She knew he was awake. Her eyes were better than his in this light, and his were open, watching her.

He would be true to Pippa. Period.

Nothing could change that rock-solid conviction.

"I'm cold," she said in a soft voice just above a whisper.

Cold? Then add another blanket, or turn the heat up.

But he didn't say that.

Because it wasn't a physical chill that had gripped her.

No, this one was spiritual. The sort of things he had been grappling with for four days, lost on an alien adventure in a land he had never dreamt of.

Gareth was fully dressed, except for his boots by the couch and his denim jacket hanging on a hook by the front door. Talyarkinash was wearing silk pajamas with a floral print on them. In the darkness, he would have guessed the fabric to be salmon, with crimson designs.

It might cover the body, but it left almost nothing about her shape to the imagination.

Still, they were both fully dressed. And it said a lot that she might trust him that much.

Gareth pulled the blanket back as an invitation for her to climb in with him.

She did, pulling the blanket around her and sliding backward into him. Gareth rolled onto his side, one arm under her head and the other wrapped around her arms to give her heat, even though he could feel the woman's warmth through the layers of clothing separating them.

After a few minutes, she fell asleep, astounding Gareth.

After another few minutes, he joined her.

PART THREE
HEROES

MORNING

GARETH AWOKE to light leaking past the curtains in the front of the flat. He was alone on the sofa, which helped. He had no idea how he would have dealt with the beautiful Nari woman waking up in his arms.

But she had wakened first and managed to slip out with rousing him. He heard her now, making tea in the kitchen, on the other side of the central wall, metal spoon clinking on a porcelain mug.

Gareth threw back the blanket and stood, taking the time to fold the thing back into a sofa and fold the blanket up.

"Gareth?" she called quietly.

"Yes, ma'am," he said.

"I'm sorry," she said. "I didn't meant to wake you."

"You didn't, I don't think," Gareth recalled. "This is my normal time to wake up."

"Tea's almost done," she appeared around the edge of the wall. "Or you can take a quick shower in the sonic fresher first."

Gareth nodded and headed to the bathroom.

That had been the single coolest thing he had found

about the *Accord of Souls*. Instead of walking naked into hot water, he could step into a small booth without taking off his clothes, just stand there for sixty seconds while the device bombarded him with some sort of sonics and radiation, then stay there while another machine vacuumed him in a way that left both him and his clothes completely clean. He hadn't even had to do laundry once since he got here.

Taking that technology home to Earth might put a lot of people out of work, but it would save so much time that everyone should come out way ahead.

The only thing that had been a problem was that he didn't have a razor. Morty had brought one before, made for a Vanir male, but they'd forgotten to stop at an all-night grocery where they could get a new one. Fortunately, his stubble was blond, so it wouldn't show up for a few days. He felt bad being out of uniform.

Except he was already out of uniform. It had been packed early, and hidden. He was undercover. Should he grow a beard?

He'd never gone more than three days without shaving, since he started.

What kind of Undercover Agent could he be, with hair already a week past the point he should have gone to the barber, and a beard?

Gareth hadn't come to any conclusion by the time he rejoined the woman scientist, but his brain was percolating like a proper coffee pot.

She must have been up for a while, because she had already gotten cleaned up and changed from her pajamas into an outfit similar to yesterdays: harem-like pants in baby blue with a lavender tunic over that, wrapped by a cute belt in black leather with all sorts of decorative, silver bangles.

She handed him a mug of steaming tea and smiled.

"How are you feeling this morning?" she asked.

"Refreshed," he discovered as he said the word.

Really spot-on. Like he had just slept twenty-four hours after eating the best ribeye possible.

"Good," she said. "Come with me."

He followed her into the bathroom. She pressed a hidden catch and the back of the linen closet opened into a hidden room beyond. They went through, and Gareth found himself back in the room with the dentist chair, but the walls were more of a brown color.

Beyond it, the same kind of control room as at her lab.

Back where her bedroom would have been, in the other apartment, a working space like what he was really expecting. Just a single workbench with the black top, scarred and stained and melted in a few places.

A computer on a desk in the corner.

Restaurant-sized refrigerators took up the whole back, three of them.

She moved around the workbench and gestured him to stand across from her.

"You here," she ordered mildly. "I need to take some blood, and then test how it will react. Take off your outer shirt, please."

She was more relaxed today. That much was obvious. Maybe it was escaping, and being saved, and escaping again. Plus a good night's sleep, even if she had to have a human to do it.

The plaid shirt in the colors of Sky Patrol came off, leaving him with only the tucked-in white t-shirt. Talyarkinash pulled some strange medical device out of a drawer and held it out. With her other hand, she grabbed his wrist and turned his arm over.

She touched the inside of his forearm briefly. It was more like a puppy's lick than anything, and then she pulled it back.

Gareth looked down and realized that it had left a tiny,

red spot. Had she just drawn blood? That painlessly? That quickly?

There was another invention to take home, if he ever could.

The machine beeped after a few seconds. Talyarkinash hmmm-ed a bit and read some readout.

Rather than speak, she put it down on the counter and began to pull vials out of the farthest-right refrigerator. From underneath Talyarkinash pulled out a small crucible and a pair of eyedroppers.

It all looked incredibly sciency.

First, she poured some of a vial into the crucible. Then she added exactly three drops from the second bottle. The second eyedropper went into the side of the first device, and came out filled with a bright red fluid.

Blood? Wow.

"Ready?" she asked, looked up at him with an unexpected smile.

Gareth smiled back and nodded.

Talyarkinash dropped a single drop of Gareth's blood into the crucible, and stirred it with a glass rod that had appeared from somewhere when he wasn't looking.

At first, it started to steam a little.

And then a lot.

Before Gareth knew what was happening, the sides of the crucible cracked and the mixture inside poured out and started to melt the surface of the counter.

When Talyarkinash managed to splash it with some fresh water from the sink, it had eaten a disk about an eighth of an inch into the surface, which looked like a plastic of some sort.

"*Fardel*," she whispered under her breath.

Gareth felt like he should blush at this point, to listen to a lady curse in public.

"Everything okay?" he ventured, unsure of his footing.

She looked up and there was almost no color in her eyes, just slitted-open irises like it was all black to bottom of her soul.

She sucked a loud breath in and blew it out.

"Had that been my blood, Gareth, or Morty's, or anybody else's, there would have been the slightest puff of steam," she explained. "Just enough to see, but you might miss it if you blinked. Normally, the second experiment is to do the same thing in a genetic spectrometer to see where we might manage adjustments, if someone had any space left."

"Okay?"

"I didn't do this with Maximus," she continued. "We were just upgrading him slightly by causing him to resize into a Vanir, so it was a simple enough cut and slice job."

"Cut and slice?" Gareth felt his hair want to stand on end.

"I program a virus like a phage, Gareth," she looked up in deadly seriousness, even if the meaning of some of the words eluded him. "Once we inject it, it infects every one of your cells and reprograms them to make you someone else. In the case of Maximus, he went to sleep for a few hours, and then ate like a horse for a week as his body suddenly grew a foot and he put on almost a hundred pounds of mass. After that, I never saw him again, but Morty and Xiomber said they did something similar to raise his IQ to genius levels."

"But we aren't stopping there," Gareth observed.

"We're not," Talyarkinash agreed nervously. "Especially with all the changes I needed to program. This goes well beyond just making you Vanir-sized, since I need to program the changes with a morphic level clear out at the limits of anything anybody has ever done."

Gareth reached out and took her hand before she could pull it back.

"This is necessary," he said. "I understand that you might kill me accidentally in the process. It might be the single dumbest idea I have ever had, but it was the only context I could find for myself to encompass what I needed to stop Marc from taking over the entire galaxy."

"Are you absolutely sure you want to do this?" she asked in a quiet voice.

"No," he said. "I'm sure it is probably suicidal. But I don't know any other way to handle it. And the clock is running."

WARLORD

"THAT FOOL SHOULD CONSIDER himself lucky that he didn't get away from the police," Marc snarled as Maiair finished her report. "He had the human dead to rights, and let Dr. Liamssen shoot him? Let him rot in prison. Make sure nobody posts bail for that fool. If someone does, I want them both brought to me in chains."

"As you command," Maiair replied, turning to signal to her younger sister with the message to convey.

Once the younger woman was gone, Marc was alone with the older in his outer chamber. He moved to the table and took a seat, gesturing for her to do the same. Normally, he would enjoy a glass of wine right now, but he was too angry for that to settle him.

This was why he needed to go get some of his old gang, even if he had to break them out of prison. He knew of the perfect tool for a jailbreak. However, right now he was surrounded by fools that would rather talk than shoot. Cleveland Eddy and Two-gun Kowalski wouldn't have made that mistake.

"What do we know about Talyarkinash Liamssen?" he asked, rubbing his eyes in frustration.

"Best in the field," Maiair replied. "At least among those willing to work for us under the table. Probable a few better geneticists out there, but not that much better."

"Make your plans on the assumption that the man coming after us is my size and at least as smart as me," Marc warned her.

"As smart?" Maiair asked.

"She's the one who did my physical structure, Maiair," Marc said. "Morty and Xiomber did the programming that upgraded my mind. At a minimum, you're now facing me, but as a cop."

"Then we might have a problem, boss," she said carefully. "You've managed to whip the rest of the gang into shape, but in doing so, you've intimidated the hell out of them. Which was a good idea at the time. Will another human echo that and cause them to freeze up? We don't know what happened to Cheepsath. He might have frozen, thinking about facing a human."

Marc sighed.

"That's my one fear here," he said. "Having to rely on a gang I didn't build, to go up against the most competent, most capable enemy I've ever known. Once I get past you, your sister, and Zorge, I'm not sure how many more managers I've got, versus a lot of make-weight street criminals."

"Managers?" Maiair asked, at a loss.

"This organization is going to have to get much bigger, Maiair," Marc replied. "And soon. We'll have to come out of the shadows at some point."

"But we are the shadows, Marc," she said, headcrest bobbing in confusion. "Why would we come out?"

"Because I've got bigger plans than just ruling *Zathus*'s

underground, Maiair," he explained. "At some point, we need to take over the whole godforsaken planet. We've already made a good start on that, with corrupt politicians we can bend."

"What's your ultimate goal, Maximus?" Maiair asked, headcrest now fully up and puffed sideways a little bit. Not challenging, but fierce.

"Taking over the entire *Accord of Souls*, Maiair," he said simply, saying it out loud for the first time.

"How in the nine hells do we do that?" she probed, headcrest puffing even more sideways with energy.

"I have a check list, actually," he said with a small laugh. "Fringe benefit of a bigger, faster brain. Who to turn. Who to kill. Things like that. At some point, I plan to import some of my old killers from Earth and their families, and start a new government."

"Would you make them Vanir, like you?" she asked carefully.

"No," Marc understood where her mind was going. "We'll leave them as humans. That way, the Vanir can still fight them on relatively even terms: Vanir might against human ruthlessness. The only real advantage the Vanir and other species will have over the next millennia will be numbers, because I won't bring that many humans over. Who knows where I'll be in a thousand years."

"Won't you be dead, Maximus?" she asked. Her headcrest had bobbed back down again. It was better than watching eyes and mouth on a human, to read their internal monolog.

"Not if all goes to plan," he explained. "The Chaa never programmed limits into humans. Why bother, since we were still stone-age cavemen, little better than animals, when they left. No, I will need a few geneticists to work on a project I have in my head, but I should be able to live forever."

"What about the rest of us?" Maiair asked.

The way she said it left a question in Marc's mind, but Maiair was a Warreth. Not the sort of creature he was interested in, except as a means to an ends.

Still, he fixed her with a stern gaze.

"You'll have as much responsibility as you can handle," he said. "For as long as you can handle it. That's decades, for your kind. I'm just sorry we can't do anything to extend that."

Her headcrest collapsed. Her head hung as well.

This creature couldn't have been hoping he would make her immortal, as well? Perhaps more? Did she think he needed a Warreth empress to rule with?

Marc's mind flitted back to the one woman who might have been a perfect queen, a decade ago. Before she made her choice. Maybe one of these days he might bring Philippa Loughty, the little maid of the lake, here, just so he could show her what a bad decision it had been, picking Gareth Dankworth over Marc Sarzynski.

If the machines were still available, he might have even chosen to bring her here now, just so she could be there when he finally caught up with the man and finished him off.

Perhaps another day.

But he would need to return home and scout for a future wife at some point. Someone he could turn into the physical form of a Vanir, while he made the changes she would need to breed up the generation of advanced humans he would need as a new nobility for the star empire he envisioned. Which he planned to rule forever.

But first, he needed the loyalty of his closest people.

"Maiair," he said softly, causing her head and headcrest to come up some. "I would grant you immortality, if I could. And we'll look into what gaps your genetic bonds have to improve you. I fear that the Warreth generally got the short end of that stick from the Chaa, along with the Tree People and the Borren. But who knows what we might be able to do with human science thrown in."

That brought some color back to her eyes. Some luster to her feathers. As much as he could do, for now.

It wouldn't do to alienate the very criminals he needed.

At least not until he didn't need them anymore.

Once he had enough humans to rule the rest, all bets were off.

SQUARE ONE

EVETH WAS BEGINNING to develop a deep and abiding antipathy towards Olehmmishqu. It was still a beautiful place, well ordered and filled with wonderfully-grand buildings and park. They were close to the river today, running down a tip that had turned out to be a miscommunication about a Moisa hairdresser. Or an old enemy with an axe to grind.

Because right now it was the people of this town that were driving her a little crazy.

Since the local police had put out a full description of the Nari scientist, Dr. Liamssen, she and Grodray had been overwhelmed with tips and leads, all of them leading to dead ends.

Grodray had made a few calls, and the Constabulary had dropped a number of officers into place around the fringes of the investigation as help, but kept things exceptionally quiet, otherwise. According to her partner, she was getting as much rope as she wanted to buy, until she decided to throw in the towel on this one.

The city was reasonably well locked down, but there were

still over three million sentient creatures to watch coming and going. Any Nari, Vanir, or Yuudixtl in an auto-taxi or taking a ferry got a second look, to make sure it wasn't one of their four quarry making a run for it. All that had happened so far was that a number of innocent civilians were being inconvenienced for reasons nobody would explain.

Most of the officers involved couldn't anyway.

Worse, the words of that dumb punk kept coming back to haunt her.

A camera on the back of a smoke shop had caught enough audio to be cleaned up and useful. The man had known about the human. And worked for someone called Maximus, which was a new name circulating, one connected with some sort of crime ring thought to operating out of *Zathus*.

And the human had a name now. *Gareth*.

But she was under observation by those same criminals. Her, personally.

Someone on the inside was feeding the thugs her itinerary. Had been for several days. Possibly, any clues that might be good ones were being filtered out by corrupt members of the local police.

Who could she trust, besides Grodray?

This Gareth fellow had tried to suggest to the crooked doctor that they were on the same side.

A human? Please. Got a sued spaceship you want to sell me?

"Let's lunch," Eveth offered as they walked out of the latest office and back onto the main street.

The river itself was two blocks over, just past a long park fronted by a variety of interesting restaurants with sidewalk dining. But she wanted an inside table today.

Grodray raised an eyebrow, but nodded and gestured for her to lead.

She found a Borren-homeworld-style café, heavy on fish in cream sauces, that had the layout she wanted. Asked for and received a booth clear at the back, as far from the restrooms as possible. Got far enough away from anyone that nobody would ever have a need to get close enough to eavesdrop.

Had even flashed her badge quietly when asking to be seated away from everyone.

It was as much privacy as she could get on short notice.

"What's up, Baker?" her partner asked as they got their orders taken.

Food wouldn't be long, as they were on the early end of lunch and had the place almost completely to themselves.

"I'm not sure our communications or our investigation are secured," she said simply.

"The information we're getting makes no sense unless someone is filtering things before they get to me. Normally, we would have several decent leads, none of which was critical, but all pointing in the same rough direction. We've gotten nothing here."

"I agree," he nodded. "Asked a few friends to look into some things without sharing with the locals."

"You think the local Constabulary is bent?" she pursued.

"No," he replied. "The police probably are, given how much underworld activity we seem to keep finding. They should have kept the place cleaner if they were doing their jobs. My gut says that we have a couple of bad apples inside our organization."

"You never listen to your gut, Grodray," she snapped.

He actually smiled at that. A twinkle came into his eyes that she had rarely seen before.

"Let's hope they believe that as much as you do, Eve," he grinned. "A reputation is a powerful thing, especially if you can lead folks astray with it. So, what do we do to shake things up?"

"I want to rattle some cages," Eveth replied. "Liamssen disappeared, which suggests that she planned ahead, and had help. We need to find who might have helped her set up her escape plans. What have we got that we could offer a low-level punk to roll on someone?"

"If we could trust the prosecutors on this planet, I would say we could offer some punks sentencing bargains for information," he noted. "But I don't know which ones are the safe ones. I can promise you that a couple of forensic accountants will be making unannounced visits in the near future."

"What do they do?" Eveth asked, lost at the term. Forensics and Accounting seemed miles apart.

"They follow money around," Grodray smiled. "How it comes in, when it comes out, where it goes, how it comes back. Most criminals aren't smart enough to hide their tracks well enough from those sorts of Prime Investigators."

Prime Investigators. The true free agents. Had her partner called in some favors from old friends at that level? Was it that necessary? Were things that bad?

Eveth wondered if the *Accord of Souls* was closer to tottering than she had ever suspected. She had always thought that crime was just a little worse than it used to be. Maybe she needed to go back generations and compare? Was that something a Prime Investigator might do?

"Okay, so we can find corrupt politicians and the people holding their puppet strings," Eveth said. "But that's still going to take months. I have a feeling we have days at most. Liamssen is a geneticist. That suggests they plan to recast their human so he can hide. What do we know about human genetics?"

Or rather, what did you know that you haven't been able

to tell me before, but which might be utterly critical right now, Jackeith?

She saw Grodray do a lot of processing quickly, from the way his eyes shifted back and forth on some invisible horizon.

Finally, those internal voices reached some consensus.

"This is Level-7 stuff, Eve," he began slowly. She nodded with the gravity of that pronouncement. "Humans are not part of the *Accord of Souls*. Were never modified by our ancestors, the Chaa. They look like smaller versions of the Vanir, *Those Left Behind*, but that's just convergent evolution, we think."

"Okay," she said, holding her breath.

"Most geneticists can work with basic things," he continued, pausing to glance over his shoulder to make sure they were along. "Fix problems at birth. Alter hair or skin or feather color. That sort of thing. Non-threatening to galactic order."

"What about the humans, Grodray?"

"There might not be *any* limitations on them, Eve," he said quietly. "They might be a blank slate onto which a geneticist with a lot of skill and no scruples might be able to paint."

"So those killers…"

"Might be turned into one of us easy enough," Grodray nodded. "Vanir are the closest match, if you want to hide. Plus you add size and mass to an already dangerous species. Look at what that human was able to do to you in his native form. Now make him my size with those muscles."

"Would she stop there?" Eveth asked.

"What do you mean?"

"Would a criminal geneticist just stop at making him Vanir, Grodray?" Eveth asked. "If there are no limits, would she go crazy? Most doctors have some level of god-complex, trying to either make the world a better place, or prove that they are smarter than everyone else. What might she do?"

Again he turned to look out of the booth. Nobody was anywhere close.

"Six months ago, we had suspicions that Cinnra, on *Zathus*, was trying to get himself a human killer," Grodray said. "Not long after that, about two months ago, Cinnra was dead and there was a new boss. One nobody had heard of before. A renegade Vanir, according the very little we've been able to piece together."

"A modified human?" she gasped.

Grodray shrugged meaningfully.

"And somebody in the gang went and got themselves a cop, to try and stop this Maximus?" Eveth leapt into the darkness. "But they'll need to upgrade him to a Vanir as well. Will they stop?"

"That's why we're functionally acting like Prime Investigators on this, Eve," her partner said, deadly serious. "Go wherever the crime takes us, without *being* Prime Investigators, because that might attract attention."

"Are you really just a Senior Constable, Jackeith Grodray?" she asked, making another intuitive leap.

Another grin. But not a no. Or a yes.

"Then we're back to the top," she said. "I don't think we have time to do anything but kick over an anthill and see what happens. If Maximus is really a disguised human, and Gareth is about to become a Vanir, we're potentially facing a war among literal gods, right here on our beat. You need to find me a door I can kick in."

His eyes got a faraway look to them, like he was checking files for the right address. Someone that wasn't normally worth rousting, or maybe a criminal he knew about, because those were easier to keep track of.

Instead of answering, he pulled out his pocketcomm and dialed.

"Yeah, me," he said to whoever answered.

Pause.

"I want a name," Grodray said. "Someone at mid-level that is wired in enough to give me the information I want when my crazy partner has him dangling out a window by one ankle."

Longer pause. Probably some hemming and hawing at the other end. Like maybe she already had that sort of reputation on *Orgoth Vortai* and someone might know that.

She had never actually let go. But it made a fantastic threat, when a woman who was bigger than you could hold you by one leg, upside down, over a thirty-foot-drop.

"And remember, you're the one signing this check," Grodray added his own threat when he got an answer.

If whoever it was wasn't on the level, Jackeith Grodray might be coming for them next. With an angry partner in tow.

Food arrived as he hung up, so he sat silently, but she could see that twinkle in his eyes again.

When they were alone, and he checked, the man smiled like a shark spying a wounded seal.

"I might have someone for you, Eve," he said.

Good.

She had to stop two gods from destroying the *Accord of Souls*. And she absolutely had to do it tonight.

AWAKENING

GARETH WAS BACK in the dentist chair. The walls were brown, so he knew he hadn't fallen into a nightmarish dream, reliving those few days in the other chair, being slowly eaten by the psionic drill.

Talyarkinash was in the other room, tuning things as well as she could.

She had gone as far as her extensive experience and creativity could take her, she had told him. And he believed her, having watched quietly all day as the woman alternatively calculated and cursed under her breath.

They both felt the pressure coming to a head. Angry people out there were looking for their scalps, and he had only one option to protect this woman who had come to trust a human.

"Gareth, are you ready?" she said over the intercom.

"I am," he said, taking a deep breath.

"Stand by."

The chair grabbed him in iron bands. Wrists, shins, chest, head. He was back in that technological iron maiden, waiting for the mad scientist to press the door shut on him.

"I wish I could say otherwise, but this is going to hurt," she offered an early apology. "Normally, we would space the six injections out over as many days, with stops to monitor your medical condition and feed you a proper, balanced diet. But as you know, they could kick in the door at any moment."

Lunch had been everything left over from dinner, plus a can of pasta and some canned fruit, until he felt like he would explode if he took another bite.

"I understand, Talyarkinash," he replied. "Thank you for doing this my way. I can handle pain. I am Earth Force Sky Patrol. There is no other choice. And if it fails, keep notes so you can fix it for the next agent you recruit, because we both know nobody in the *Accord* can stop him."

"I will, Gareth," she said quietly. "And thank you for last night. I really needed a friend."

Gareth started to say something. Started to blush. But she must have hit the button as she spoke, because something tapped him on the left shoulder, the one closer to the heart, and suddenly his entire body was on fire.

He might have screamed. Wanted to. Told his lungs and throat to carry through, but his body was no longer his to command.

Instead, Gareth was composed of a roaring fire that someone else was trying to extinguish with acid. Every nerve. Every muscle. Every neuron.

Gareth could never remember experiencing a tenth, even a hundredth as much pain. Diving across death pressure without a helmet, in order to save the ship from detonation, hadn't hurt as much.

His eyes were on fire now, or perhaps his optic nerves were slowly being eaten by miniature piranha, one angry bite at a time.

After an eternity measured in the lifetime of stars, the pain seemed to ebb.

Gareth found he could think again. His throat was raw, but that might have been the screaming he was hoping he was able to do. His arms and legs felt like wet spaghetti sliding off a plate.

"Gareth?" the Angel of Death called his name. "Can you hear me?"

No, not the Angel of Death. Retribution, perhaps.

That would make her *Nemesis*, the bringer of retribution. Except that was his job.

The helmet retracted and Gareth found that he could see again.

He looked up and saw Talyarkinash's azure eyes staring down at him with concern.

Yes, he had become Nemesis. That would in turn make her the goddess of night, Nyx.

He rather enjoyed that thought.

"Are you okay?" she seemed to be asking.

Gareth nodded and grunted, not quite willing to trust his tongue right now.

"Good," she continued. "Because somebody just kicked in the door to my apartment, across the hallway. We've run out of time."

CLOSING THE TRAP

"WE'VE GOT THEM," she said as Marc let Maiair into the other chamber.

Yooyar was with her, and both had their headcrests at full display. Marc was pretty sure what that signified among the Warreth, but now was really not the time.

"Where?" he asked. "And are you sure?"

There had been a couple of false alarms so far today. Those two Constables were getting progressively less communicative with the local cops, which suggested that they had finally figured out what was wrong. Probably, they were on the verge of cleaning up the local police and Constabulary, which would seriously dent his operations on this planet, but that was a problem for tomorrow.

Today, he needed to kill Gareth Dankworth. After that, he had time to put longer-term plans into action.

"We leaned extra heavy on someone who should have told us sooner," Yooyar said with the sort of grim tone that suggested she just might be capable of killing in cold blood, which made her a rarity in the *Accord of Souls*. If she could do that, he would have as much work for the young Warreth as she wanted to undertake. "When we threatened to hand him over to the cops, he gave us an address. Supposedly, around two years ago Liamssen hired him to build her a secret lab not far from the university campus."

"Good," Marc exclaimed. "If it really is the place, then we'll turn him over to the Constables later for holding out on us now. If not, I want you to kill him. I'm done playing around and the stakes are too high right now."

"Who do we take with us?" Maiair asked the million-credit-question.

Who did he trust, when he was about to take on a human? Maiair had been right. Most of the team he brought to *Hurquar* were only really dangerous to their own kind, those inside the *Accord of Souls*.

What he really needed were killers. Men he had used back on Earth.

This group would have to do.

"Get me a driver who knows his stuff," Marc commanded. "You two, plus Zorge. Bring stunners only, as I may need to torture information out of the four of them later, and I want them all alive for now."

Yooyar nodded and departed. Maiair waited an extra second, as if about to say something, before she nodded and departed as well.

The way the women had reacted to the word *torture* just exacerbated the difference between the human, ruling caste he would need to build later, and the pitiful pacifists that had inherited the galaxy from those people who really should have done something about humans fifty thousand years ago.

That, or they needed to come back now and set it to right.

The failure of the Chaa to stop him was evidence enough to Marc that he was indeed destined to live forever and rule the galaxy as a newly-born god.

ANT HILLS

EVETH HAD TAKEN the time to change before they set out. She was back in the blue-gray bodysuit, covered over with armored scales and sporting a holster for her pistol on her left thigh. The blue ring over her heart seemed to be filling her with white-hot plasma from the surface of a star. Grodray had changed too, but he had gone the full route, including the white, dress beret and tunic over the top of his armor, so that made him look like the good cop.

That was okay. Eveth was angry enough already. And Grodray had said they were acting as Prime Inspectors on this case. That meant she had a great deal more leeway on rules and regulations than a mere Constable.

Time to put that to the test.

The auto-taxi had dropped them on a side street not far from the main tourist area, down by the river. They had eaten lunch not a mile from here, but by night it was an entirely different world.

Neon signs competed for attention Music pulsed a low, rumbling bass she could feel in her sternum, even from here. There was a line of people at the door, waiting for one of the bouncers protecting the joint to let them in, assuming they passed the requisite coolness test inherent in clubs like this.

"That's it?" she asked, nodding the direction of the target as they came around the corner. The music hit her like a wet towel.

Grodray just nodded.

"What exactly are you planning to do, Eve?" he asked in a simple voice, falling into stride with her as she moved.

"Kick over an anthill, Jack," she smiled back, almost biting her lip with anticipation.

No more deduction. No more intuitive leaps into the darkness. Just heads that needed cracking together.

She approached the line and went around the rope holding the unwelcome at bay.

Two of the bouncers in black shirts at the front door were Nari. Big specimens of determination that probably intimidated the hell out of tourists and artists. The one in the middle was a Vanir. He was maybe Grodray's height, and had lots of mass, but much of it was turning into a pot belly around the middle.

Eveth flashed her badge as she got close and slipped it into her thigh holder so it was out of the way and her hands were clear.

"You can't go in there," the fat guy said. "It's a private party."

"Stop me then," Eveth said.

Apparently, they bred them dumb on *Hurquar*, or wherever this guy was from. He actually reached out and tried to grab Eveth's shoulder as she walked by him.

It had been a day. A whole week of days like this.

Eveth grabbed the hand on her right shoulder with her own right hand. She twisted it forward hard as she kept walking, forcing him sideways and down if he didn't want his arm broken.

One of the two Nari looked like he might want to cause trouble, until a stun pistol appeared in his face, at the other end of a long, Vanir arm belonging to her angry partner.

"Official business," he said, invoking the kinds of dread-bringing words that would get the other two thrown in jail for weeks until Grodray or Eveth decided they had suffered enough embarrassment.

Interfering with a Constabulary investigation was a felony everywhere, just for situations like this.

Both Nari turned white around the eyes. Ears went flat against skulls and the two men backed away.

Eveth would have expected to see tails tucked under, if they weren't wearing baggy pants.

She turned her attention to the big guy, still trying not to have a broken arm. He had a look about him of a bully boy. Just the kind of guy you wanted at the front door of a club like this. She twisted a little more, and he was on his knees.

Eveth pulled her spare handcuffs from a belt pouch and hooked this bastard to the door handle. The only way he was going anywhere without her now involved a cutting laser, patience, and a high pain threshold.

Grodray nodded his approval.

Inside, the wall of sound was almost a painful experience. Eveth wondered what subsonics might be bathing the crowd in emotional manipulation, but it wasn't her problem.

She looked to the right, and saw a crowd pressed up against a long bar like a rising tide. On the left, tables filled with sweaty patrons. In the middle, a dance floor and a light show so bright it might constitute an optical assault.

The door she wanted was on the far side, back on the left, near where risers went up to tables in the back with a good view.

Two more goons protected it as she wended her way through the mob, not exactly elbowing folks out of her way, but taking full advantage of the smaller species around her, who couldn't resist her angry mass.

Another Nari guarded this door, with a Grace on the other side. Both wore the same black shirt of security employees, and had noted her approach with concern bordering on hostility.

Eveth smiled as she got close enough for the men to move to block the door. With one hand, she flipped open the wallet with the badge. With the other, she drew her pistol and pointed it at the one on the left. Grodray's pistol was there a split-second later, like he had known how this was going down.

Maybe he secretly was a Prime Investigator, hiding out with the little people?

"Your choice," Eveth yelled over the music.

The Grace nodded and backed down first, sliding across from the doorway and more or less pushing the Nari against the wall and whispering something in his ear as he did.

Like what a really bad idea it might be to resist the angry, giant woman with a badge and a gun.

Through the door the sound fell to a dull echo in the middle distance. The walls were rough wood covered over with old concert playbills, and the floor badly scuffed tile. Eveth passed a kitchen that extended behind the wall on the bar side, and then a blank space that was probably the back of the restrooms.

The hallway ended in a wooden door, older than the hills, and with a name on it in gold letters. The name Grodray had gotten for her earlier.

She had always wanted to do this, but it had never been an option, even in this line of work.

Without breaking stride, she stepped up and kicked the handle with all the anger she had accumulated since she came to this planet, shattering the strike panel out of the frame and a good chunk of wood from the door.

Inside, a fat Grace was talking on the telephone and looked up with a surprise that turned his tentacles nearly white.

"I'll call you back," he said. "Something just came up."

The rest of the office was empty. Just the short, fat man behind a battered desk, two chairs, and wall-to-wall pictures of famous people who had been here or played the club at some point in their careers.

Eveth still had the gun in her hand, so she sat in the nearer chair and smiled at him.

"I want information," she said primly. "You have three options. One: you can just tell me what I need. Two: you end up spending the rest of the night and maybe a week or two in jail while badly-misfiled paperwork gets untangled."

Pause.

"What's option number three," he asked, falling for it like any good straight man.

"You have to stop at the hospital first," she smiled.

CONFRONTATION

GARETH WAS in no shape to fight, but he had no choice. He stumbled upright as Talyarkinash put his arm around her neck and wobbled with him towards the door.

A crash nearby signaled the secret door being broken open, and suddenly there were people pointing guns at him.

Gareth tried to manage his drunkenness, but his body was only vaguely under his control at this point. He recognized two Warreth females, both holding what looked like stun pistols pointed at he and Talyarkinash. Both women were cherry-red, with the taller one having black and white highlights and the shorter one having mostly yellow underplummage.

A Vanir male entered a second later. He was magnificent. At least seven-foot-four and built like a linebacker. Handsome face with dark, curly hair covering the man's head. He seemed to be familiar.

"It looks like we're too late to stop *her* from upgrading you," the man said in a cruel voice. "But that just means that I'm not too late to stop *you*."

He smiled down at Gareth, but it was more of a sneer.

After a moment, Gareth finally recognized the man. The scale had thrown him off.

Intellectually, he had known it was a fact, but coming face to face with it was something entirely else.

"Hello, Marc," Gareth said slowly, trying to sound more coherent than he was. "Or should I call you Maximus now?"

"Either will work, old friend," Gareth's worst nightmare smiled. "Welcome to the *Accord of Souls*."

And then the bastard shot him.

OVERLORD

MARC SMILED as the bolt took Dankworth square in the chest. For good measure, he shot the woman as well. Stunners were a cheap way to handle prisoners.

"Find the other two," he ordered brusquely.

It became clear within moments that Morty and Xiomber weren't anywhere in the suite of rooms, and there were no more hidden doors to blow open. Nothing but this operating theater, a control room, and a small lab, and no indication a pair of Yuudixtl had ever been in here.

In a way, that made it worse, because it suggested that those two knew he was going to catch up with Liamssen and Dankworth, and had already moved on, probably hoping to find another Field Agent from Earth Force Sky Patrol, or maybe even a Special Agent.

He couldn't put any of his other plans into action until he had cauterized this wound. And now he might have to start over.

How long had those two been planning to betray him?

"The place is empty, Maximus," Maiair confirmed. "What's next?"

"You two grab her," he said, pointing at the doctor on the floor of the operating theater. "Bring her along to the truck. I only gave them a medium stun, but they won't be conscious for at least thirty or forty minutes. Then I need to know where the other two are."

"What about the human?" Yooyar asked.

"I'll bring him myself," Marc said.

It was almost like picking up a ten-year-old child, using his enhanced muscles to lift up the man who had once been his best friend and toss Dankworth over a shoulder in a fireman's carry.

"What about the rest?" Maiair pressed.

Marc looked around at the space. There was no way to hide the kicked in front door of the other suite, nor the destroyed hidden door between the two flats. It would only be a matter of time until someone called the police, and the place would be crawling with badges.

Still, he had the doctor. He could get what he wanted out of her before he killed her. And still had enough connections to the authorities to get copies of her files once the police impounded them. He was pretty sure all of the corrupt locals he owned would be in jail fast enough as a result of this fiasco, but not before he could get that much out of them.

"Leave it," he decided. "I've got what I really need."

The girls were gone first, lugging the Nari traitor between them. Zorge was covering the front door when Marc emerged from the bathroom with his own burden.

"So that's him?" Zorge tsked. "Doesn't look like much."

"Neither would you, stunned," Marc snapped. "This man, this human, is orders of magnitude more dangerous than you ever dreamed of being, Zorge. He might be the only person in the universe that could stop me."

"Why haven't you killed him, then?" the spymaster asked abruptly.

"I need to know what he knows first," Marc promised. "After that, it's a whole different ballgame."

GETAWAY

MARC'S TRUCK was right where he had left it, double-parked in a loading zone at the bottom of the short tower. The *Accord* wasn't big on personally-owned vehicles, but there were always a few, so most buildings dedicated a couple of floors of the big towers to landing bays.

He had brought a simple panel truck tonight, painted on the outside with the name and phone number of a local plumbing service as a way to vanish into the scenery. Let the fools drive around in big, black limousines that screamed "*I'm important. Somebody arrest me!*"

He would settle for a quiet time in the shadows, building his power up until he could simply explode out and take what he wanted. Liamssen's notes on what she had done to Dankworth would be invaluable for that.

What little extra did they think would give that man the edge he needed to take on Maximus?

The girls were carrying the rogue geneticist towards the back of the truck as he approached. Zorge had gone ahead and was sitting up front with the driver for the word to move.

Lights suddenly appeared at the near edge of the garage as an auto-taxi landed and deposited two figures on the balcony apron outside. Something about them just had Marc's hackles up, so he crouched down, carefully setting Dankworth's body behind a window-washing repulsor craft.

The two were Vanir, and the way the female walked just screamed *cop* as Marc watched. When she passed into the internal light from the darkness outside, Marc also saw the badge on her chest.

For a moment, his rage burned crimson at the thought he had been betrayed by someone in his organization, but he stopped himself cold. Cops looking for him would have surrounded the building with heavy teams and be storming the place right now, so maybe they had just gotten lucky tip and arrived too late to keep him from his prize?

"You there," the woman cop yelled as she saw Maiair and Yooyar, carrying a body between them in unfortunate circumstances. "Stop and hands in the air. Police!"

One of the reasons Marc had chosen a Vanir as his final form, in addition to the amazing physical size, were the reflexes.

Warreth were gliders, with human-like upper arms that had been extended and flattened into wings that ran along past their hands. They were more like bats that way, and couldn't truly fly, not like the Elohynn. But that latter race was a true hexapod, a body that could usually pass for human in dim light, plus wings like an angel, except they hinged down instead of up.

The two Vanir cops had guns out and pointed before either sister could even consider dropping their package. Zorge was up front, probably with the door closed. He would suddenly find a stunner in his ear, if he wasn't paying attention.

And the cops were coming up at a bad angle for anyone in the cab to see them before it was too late.

Good thing Marc was sneakier than everyone else.

He pulled out his pistol and adjusted it to the highest settings. The beam attenuated with distance, and this would be a pretty long shot for a hand-held stunner. But he only needed to soften them up enough that they couldn't evade follow-up shots.

"What's going on here?" the woman cop yelled in an angry voice as she closed.

Her partner was a few steps back and to one side, concentrating on the rest of the garage and possible ambushes. Like Marc.

He decided to take the male first, trusting that he had enough cover to protect himself from the female cop. Yooyar would also be able to get involved if the cop stopped covering her.

Marc stayed perfectly still, aware that Vanir, like humans, had eyesight keyed to motion and color. He measured the shot in his head and watched the two cops come to rest, too far away for the sisters to attack them, but close enough to track everything happening with the truck.

The male risked a glance the other direction.

Marc exploded into motion, raising his pistol into view and triggering the shot almost before he had the barrel down, trusting that the gun itself needed a fraction of a second from the trigger pull to the primary coil energizing. About the same amount of time it took a bullet to exit a barrel under the high pressure of burning cordite.

The shot was a little high, but still tagged the male cop in the shoulder. Hopefully, it would be enough, because Marc was already tracking on the woman.

She was spinning in his direction, targeting on sound as her eyes searched for him.

Time slowed to molasses on a Nova Jersey winter day.

Marc fired.

She fired.

Marc felt the brush of her stunner, like the kiss of a tree branch whipping by, but most of it went into the vehicle in front of him. Still, his eyesight grayed out for a moment.

He fired a second shot blind. Memory said he had gotten her harder than she had gotten him, with that first shot, but he had never seen anyone with reflexes as good as his.

He needed an Empress like her, one of these days, but a modified human. Still, he had a pattern upon which to base that future wife, if he got out of this situation alive.

A third shot rang out as Marc's vision cleared.

A fourth.

Silence.

Marc managed to make out the scene.

The cop was unconscious. Both cops.

Maiair had gotten her pistol out and taken both cops down by herself, once he had distracted them.

Marc made a note to pay better attention to the older Warreth sister. She was making herself look better and better as a potential second-in-command for the organization, just as her younger sister was turning into a dangerous gunsel.

Maybe he really did need a harem after all, as a way to bind them more fully to the throne he intended to create.

"Good job," Marc said as he holstered his pistol and gathered up Dankworth's body.

"What do we do with them?" Maiair asked, covering them with her pistol anyway.

"Bring them along," Marc decided. "If they're here, there's a leak in the organization, and we need to plug it. I'll find out what they know before we work on the other two."

Marc deposited the Field Agent into the back of the van as Zorge emerged, eyes wide with surprise.

"What happened?" he asked.

"You missed all the fun, old man," Yooyar's sarcastic tones could have been used to paint a building.

"Constables?" Zorge inspected them as he helped Maiair lift the female. "How'd they find us?"

"That's your job, Zorge," Marc said coldly. "Find out who talked and have them brought to me for punishment."

"Yes, sir," the Nari spymaster nodded.

Marc pulled the unconscious male to the van and then lifted him inside, noting that the man was skinny, but still a solid block of mass. Older cop, wearing the insignia of a Senior Constable, what Marc would have called Detective Sergeant back home,

Nothing else was moving in the garage.

Before they lifted off, Marc pulled the pocketcomms from both cops and tossed them under a nearby car, aware of how easily they could be tracked, if someone was suspicious. The rest of their belongings went into a sack someone had grabbed: guns, badges, wallets, handcuffs.

Accord cops used cuffs that keyed on bio-signature, rather than the old-fashioned iron key. Marc assumed that a competent cop would put herself and her partner into the tiny, electronic brain, so using their own cuffs on them was a mere annoyance, rather than a useful tool.

Still, they would be out for a while. Long enough to get back to the warehouse he had been using as a base.

After that, he would have all the time in the world, and all sorts of interesting tools, to torture these four for all the information they had, like squeezing a sponge completely dry, before he discarded them onto the ashheap of history.

PRISONER

GARETH WOKE TO PAIN. Millions of microscopic ants marching through his veins, biting him with every stride. Hot coals scorching his flesh on a slow smoker.

A groan escaped his lips.

"Ah, you are awake, my old friend," Marc Sarzynski's voice intruded on Gareth's nightmare.

He tried to open his eyes, but the light in here stabbed his brain with icepicks.

Gareth squinted to the merest slits and tried to focus on something beyond the torture in his soul.

"Too bright?" Marc asked.

Gareth groaned again and nodded. Tried to. He wasn't sure how much of what was happening in his mind made it to the nerves and muscles of his body.

Sudden darkness reached out and embraced him in coolness.

"Better?" Marc asked. "I remember when I first awakened, as the growth began to hit. Everything hurt and I was nearly blind."

"Thank you," Gareth managed to slur out.

"Anything for my oldest, dearest friend," Sarzynski sneered. "We want you comfortable for what comes next."

Gareth heard the emphasis on that last word and knew what Maximus had planned.

He had failed. They had been too late to get everything done and escape.

Or rather, Talyarkinash had done everything she could, but Gareth had needed more time for it to happen.

Time he had run out of.

Gareth managed to open his eyes enough to see, this time. Through the fire in his body, he understood that he was hanging from a pair of manacles holding his arms up, those in turn attached to an I-beam running horizontally on some sort of frame. Another pair gripped his ankles.

The space smelled like a shipping warehouse, all dusty and oils and dry. The ceiling was far overhead, with a crane on rails up there for lifting things out of railroad cars, just like home.

Gareth was on his knees, so he fought with his body to stand. It was like lifting the old Empire State Building, but he managed, hanging forward on the chains to find his balance and drive upwards.

He couldn't stand right now. Not really.

But he wasn't about to be on his knees for Marc Sarzynski.

A breath pulled down into the base of his stomach seemed to quell some of the fires coursing through his blood. His mind might have even cleared a little.

Gareth focused on breathing and learning to think again. This was worse than the hardest concussion he had ever sustained, and his head was ringing like a church bell in synch with his heart.

"My," Sarzynski exclaimed. "You do look better already."

Gareth managed to turn his head far enough to find

Maximus, seated on a chair on a small platform, like a king on his throne. The rest of the royal suite stood around him, arrayed in layers of power and access, from the dumbest rookies at the edge of the crowd to the two Warreth women standing closest to Marc, the taller one whispering in his ear.

Gareth looked down and realized his favorite cowboy outfit was gone. Hopefully not destroyed, since he wasn't sure who that tailor had been and wanted to go back soon for more wardrobe.

In its place, Gareth was wearing a long robe of a heavy, white linen. It hung long on his feet and wrists, as if it were for a Vanir, rather than a human. The white suggested something angelic, which was probably appropriate, given the roles he and Marc had chosen to play.

But the oversized nature also sent an important message. Sarzynski understood. Knew that Gareth would be growing as the various viruses worked their way through his body, reprogramming things and triggering all manner of changes. Hopefully, he would miss the important changes when focusing on the obvious.

"Are you ready to talk yet?" Marc asked a polite, even pleasant voice. "The others haven't woken up yet, so I can't put them to the question and find out what they know."

"Why, Marc?" Gareth asked simply, as he managed to gain control of his mouth.

"Power, Gareth," the man replied. "You had always managed to thwart me, back home, mister White Knight on a Charging Steed. Here, we are a whole new thing, and the *Accord of Souls* lacks the fundamental tools to prevent me from taking over."

"Emperor Marc the First?" Gareth asked sarcastically.

"Indeed, old friend," the criminal overlord smiled grandly. "I had even considered who I might need for an Empress…"

The way he left the phrase dangling left no doubt in Gareth's mind as to whom Marc was referring.

"If you hurt her…"

"Relax, Dankworth," Marc said. "She made her choice, and I honor that. She'll make a lovely little housewife for you. Or would have. I will need a woman with grander dreams to create a new species of rulers here."

Gareth had a better view of the crowd than Marc did. He watched the implications of those words ripple out, a pebble dropped into a still pond. Useful information, long term, but Gareth didn't know how long he had. That Sarzynski hadn't killed him already meant that there was something the man needed to know, and needed Gareth to supply it.

Knowing Maximus, the man would resort to torture at some point. Gareth steeled his soul to resist as long as he could.

Another deep breath and the fires seemed to bank, turning down to a small hearth of coals, just keeping him warm on a chill night rather than threatening him with a foretaste of hell.

"So what do you want, Marc?" Gareth even managed to sound calm, he thought.

"I want to watch you change, Gareth," the man replied with a smile. "See what *she* did to you, so I can figure out what I might want to add to the current repertoire."

Gareth followed Marc's eyes and saw Talyarkinash strapped down to a chair off to one side, head lolling as she was still out cold. Beyond her, a pair of Vanir in steel-blue uniforms. Gareth looked close and recognized Constable Baker and her partner, also captured.

Only the brothers seemed to have escaped. Hopefully, they had enough money and connections to remain at large while they assembled another wormhole generator and sought more help. Nobody else in the *Accord of Souls* was left who could stop this madman.

"She made me a match for you, Marc," Gareth said gruffly, turning his eyes back to his foe. "That's what the *Accord of Souls* needed, after all. Someone who could stand in your path and say *No*."

"Well, then you both failed," Marc said. "Not even the strength of Samson will save you now. I will cut your hair and blind you, so you can listen to the others spill their secrets first, and then their blood."

"Marc, you can just walk away, you know," Gareth retorted quietly. "Take your little mob of pitiful losers and vanish back into the shadows. I'll even give you a head start."

"You think I should fear you, little human?" Marc voice suddenly turned to rage.

"Because if you hurt her, or the Constables, I promise that there will be no place in the galaxy or in hell that will save you from my wrath."

"You don't seem to understand, Dankworth," Marc's anger towered as high as the great ceiling overhead. "I've been waiting for this moment for years. I was always second best when you were around. Anything I did was almost, but not quite as good, as the great Gareth St. John Dankworth of the Earth Force Sky Patrol. Have you any idea what that's like?"

"I wasn't competing with you, Marc," Gareth said simply. "I was simply trying to do the best I could. Trying to make the Solar System a better place. I will do the same with the *Accord of Souls*, since I can never go home now."

"Fool," Sarzynski thundered. "You'll be dead."

Gareth watched him rise from the cheap, imported throne, just an over-sized metal chair, and stomp down to ground level. The criminal gang around him had already fallen silent. Now they parted like the waters at his approach.

Maximus came close, but not close enough for Gareth to grab him. Still, Gareth got his first major shock. Marc Sarzynski was only half a head taller now, so Gareth had reached something like six-foot-nine as his body expanded under the force of all the chemicals and transformational virii.

A hunger took root at the bottom of Gareth's soul, but it wasn't just for nourishment.

This one was for justice.

"Now, you will watch what your foolhardy gambles have brought," Marc snarled.

It felt like they were the only two people in the entire vast auditorium of the warehouse, the rest of the people hanging silent on pins and needles.

Gareth watched his foe stomp over to where Talyarkinash was strapped to the chair. A nearby table had been covered with a cloth, one that Marc pulled back now and cast from him.

Underneath, what looked to Gareth like the contents of surgical theater had been laid out in careful order. Gareth felt his stomach clench.

"Do I have your attention, Dankworth?" Sarzynski yelled angrily.

Without pausing for a response, Marc reached down and picked something up. Gareth struggled against the chains binding him as Marc stepped around behind the Nari woman, but the criminal did not touch her.

Instead, he snapped something and held it under her nose. Even from here, Gareth picked up the rank assault of the smelling salts.

Talyarkinash moaned and stirred, struggling weakly and vainly against the ties binding her to the chair.

"Good," Marc said in a cruel voice. "You're awake, Dr. Liamssen."

It dawned on Gareth that he had never heard the woman's last name, having been apparently on a first-name basis with her from the first moment. He would apologize to her later for his social failures.

"Whaa…" Talyarkinash fumbled to find a context.

"Welcome to *my* lab, traitor," Marc continued. "I'm going to ask you questions, and you are going to answer them. If you don't, I am going to use pain as a tool and an art form to slowly rip away your sanity, until I get what I want. If you please me, I might kill you quickly."

"MAXIMUS!" Gareth roared across the space. "This is your last warning."

"YOU DO NOT GIVE ME ORDERS, HUMAN!" Marc screamed back in a voice of cruelty that transcended human or Vanir.

Gareth watched the man pick up something from the table and step around behind the woman again, so Gareth that had an unobstructed view.

"My friend needs to understand his situation, doctor," Marc hissed. "And I need you to understand that your only choice now is how much pain you will suffer before you tell me what I want to know."

Gareth growled, low in his chest, as Marc held out the thing to Talyarkinash's left arm. It was a fine-pointed, surgical knife, but Gareth wasn't sure how he knew that from this far away. It should have appeared as a steel pencil, considering the distance.

"We begin," Marc said in a voice dripping with venom.

He took the knife and turned it sideways.

Talyarkinash struggled, but she was bound too effectively to move anything but her ears.

Slowly, Marc ran it down the outside of her arm in a move that made no sense, until Gareth saw her fur fall away in a strip an inch wide and several inches long.

He and Marc locked eyes across the space for a moment, rage swirling back and forth like a storm's tide. Lightning bolts of fury seemed to pass between them, at least in Gareth's imagination

Marc turned the blade again and plunged it directly into Talyarkinash's arm, right in the center of the bald spot, dragging it far enough to make a deep cut. Bright red blood welled up and began to drip.

Talyarkinash whimpered in pain.

Gareth saw more red, but this time it was in his soul. Anger, previously banked, waited no more. Those coals, calm and waiting at the center of his being, they were no longer quiet. Hot wind blasted them and they exploded into the sort of white heat necessary to forge steel.

The pain Gareth felt was worse than anything he had previously endured, but this was driven by wrath, not confusion.

Gareth squinted his eyes and howled. Felt the sound echo off the far walls of the warehouse as Marc smiled at him, pulling the blade free and wiping it clean on Talyarkinash's tunic.

Gareth looked at his left hand now, the manacled arm closer to the heart, where six injections had forever altered his life.

Nothing would alter his soul, but the flesh of his hand seemed to melt under his gaze, showing the faintest tint of bronze as his fingers extended a little in the fury of a molten forge.

He looked back up at Marc and smiled.

Something had changed in the man's face. Fear, perhaps, had taken root and begun to spread its tendrils.

"What are you doing?" Marc called in a voice twinged now with doubt, supplanting the towering anger that had been there a moment ago.

"Being born," Gareth said simply.

He closed his eyes and reached down into the depths of his soul, plunging both hands into that pile of white-hot coals, seeking something. What he wasn't sure.

Perhaps Excalibur.

Gareth had been raised on all the great martial tales of history: Arthur who was known as Pendragon. Saint George of Lydda, reputed to have slain a dragon, and Theodore of Amasea, another warrior for his faith. But others as well, including Bilbo who fought a dragon in his own way and lived to tell the tale.

All throughout the Western Literary canon were sprinkled great beasts who tormented men. Creatures known as dragons that had become receptacles of dreams of flight and fancy, powerful immortals who challenged men spiritually as often as they did martially. Symbols as well as monsters.

Gareth had no desire to face Samson's fate, even as he considered the manacles binding his arms and legs to an iron frame. Nor would he accept the imagery of another man so bound, with the Spear of Longinus plunged into his side.

There was only one God, according to Pastor Jacob, and Gareth lacked the arrogance to challenge that notion, even as the desperate, criminal scientists of the *Accord of Souls* sought to make him over into one.

But he would accept a dragon as a powerful totem.

Gareth howled again as the fire crept out of his soul and immolated his physical form, Talyarkinash's greatest success coming to flesh and fruition around him.

Dragonsong.

But this roar was not pain.

No, this was retribution.

Gareth turned his face on the rest of Marc's gang and

snarled his rage at them, watching them shrink beneath him as he did.

Except that they were staying the same size.

Gareth was growing. Elongating.

Transforming.

The four manacles shattered as he flexed mighty limbs, covered over now with bronze scales inspired by two scared Yuudixtl scientists, willing to risk everything to undo the evil they had unleashed on the galaxy.

Reptilian Pandoras trying to find Hope at the last.

Marc Sarzynski stood frozen in shock as he watched.

Gareth leapt into the air, trusting the instincts Talyarkinash had programmed as mighty wings unfolded from his back and began to beat. A tail swished behind him like a great rudder as he was suddenly airborne, racing towards the suddenly low-hanging ceiling overhead.

A sound below drew his attention. A stunner pistol firing. At him.

The range was too great for such a small weapon to be effective, but both of the Warreth women would not let that dissuade them. They continued to fire. A gray-furred Nari male joined in after a second.

Gareth had no interest in finding out if the weapons would stun his new form, but he also didn't want to simply annihilate them all, as much as the beast in his breast called for it.

He banked at the far end of the warehouse and set his eyes on the array of species representing Sarzynski's gang. Wings beat a tattoo on the sky and he dove, weaving back and forth to avoid the fire.

He would not kill them unnecessarily. Fear of dragons was a thing all humans seemed to be born with. Gareth hoped that these other species, who had already learned to fear a human, might acquire an even greater fear of a dragon.

He took a breath and opened his mouth, screaming pure fury at them like a physical assault.

Dragonfear.

They broke, scattering in mindless panic as they tried to find a door out of the building.

Anything to escape their worst nightmare made flesh before their very eyes.

"GARETH!" Marc screamed as Gareth pivoted on a wing and began a second pass.

Gareth found the man. He had not moved at all, except to grab Talyarkinash by the fur on the back of her head and pull it back to expose her throat.

"I'll kill her," he warned, almost touching her with the tip of that scalpel.

Gareth swung around in a tight arc, watching the rest of the gang flee, including the three with enough anger to shoot before. Just to make a point, he picked out a spot, high on a nearby wall, and trusted Talyarkinash again.

Fire erupted from his open snout, a great gout of flames that licked the wall and scorched it down to the metal in an instant, raising the temperature in the room several degrees as metal oxidized under that assault.

The rabbits ran even harder.

Gareth turned his attention back to Marc, holding a hostage he would kill, even knowing that Gareth could immolate him a moment later.

It was time to talk, finally.

Gareth circled one last time and swooped in to land, nowhere close to the one known as Maximus and his hostage, but instead crushing Marc's throne under the immense weight of a twenty-meter-long dragon. One of mankind's greatest terrors, soon to be something the criminals of the *Accord of Souls* learned to fear as well.

He felt his tail flicker angrily behind him, knocking

things over with a variety of sounds. Rear paws had grown talons, which he dug into the wood of the small stage, splintering it loudly. Front paws came down and flexed as well. His wings folded to half-mast, not retracted, but not spread to full extension.

"What have you done?" Marc screamed, almost mindlessly.

"She made me into something that could stop you, Marc," Gareth said in a voice that sounded like his own, down an entire octave of resonance and anger.

"You're no longer human," the man raged, amazed.

"Nor are you, Maximus," Gareth replied coldly. "Remember that. You have chosen to become a Vanir, among your other enhancements. You are no longer human either."

Gareth let his weight settle forward, like a cat resting, except he kept all four paws out for quick movement. His eyes had enough peripheral vision to see nearly the entire space of the warehouse behind him. He watched the last three, the dangerous criminals: the two Warreth and Nari, get to an outside door and flee into the night without once looking back.

Let them go. They had the fear of a dragon carved into their souls now. As he had intended from the start. They would take that with them and infect the entire underground with it, fighting half of his future battles for him.

"Stay back," Marc threatened, jerking Talyarkinash's head hard enough to elicit another yelp of pain from her. "I'm warning you."

"I will make you a deal, Marc," Gareth rumbled. "Put the knife down without hurting her and walk away. If you do not, you will never make it out of this building alive. But I will let you go, right now."

"Let me go?" Marc's mind seemed to have snapped. "What kind of a deal is that?"

"I will make you that promise on my honor, Marc Sarzynski," Gareth said. "For old times' sake. We were both members of the Earth Force Sky Patrol, once upon a time. You know what my word is worth."

"Just walk away?" Marc asked, sanity creeping slowly back into his voice. "Just like that?"

"Just like that, Marc," Gareth promised. "Tomorrow, I will begin to hunt you again, in earnest, but today you and your kind are free to go. The price is the lives of Talyarkinash Liamssen and the two Constables."

"Your word?"

"Yes, Marc," Gareth acknowledged.

Talyarkinash hissed in surprise when Marc Sarzynski suddenly let go of her hair. Gareth watched him step to the table and replace the knife he had picked up earlier, grabbing a bandage and strapping it around the oozing wound in the woman's left arm.

Marc reached down and undid one of the straps holding her in place, freeing her right arm. He placed her hand over the bandage, so she could hold it in place.

Gareth held his breath as Marc Sarzynski, the criminal mastermind known as Maximus, turned to face him one last time.

"Until tomorrow, Gareth," he nodded.

"Until tomorrow, Marc," Gareth replied.

The Vanir warrior, who had once been his best friend, when they were both humans, turned and began to walk away.

"That's it?" a new voice raged into the empty silence.

Gareth and Marc both turned to Constable Baker, apparently awake now. She must have been silently biding her time, but Gareth could understand.

"That's it, Eveth Baker," Marc said.

He turned and quickly made his way to an exit.

215

"You're letting him go?" she turned and directed her bile up at Gareth.

"For now," Gareth reassured her as the door slammed shut on Marx Sarzynski.

Carefully, he made his way down from the platform, kicking the uncomfortable, crushed remains of Sarzynski's throne to one side as he did.

Gingerly, he reached out a giant paw and tugged as the bindings holding Talyarkinash to the chair, snapping them with the razor edge of his talon.

"It worked," she said with an awe-tinged voice. "Thank you for saving my life."

"No, Talyarkinash Liamssen," Gareth replied. "Thank you for saving mine."

"Release me," Eveth Baker demanded as Talyarkinash rose and hugged Gareth's serpentine neck with her good arm. "That bastard's getting away."

Gareth turned to the female officer, noting with interest that both of them were awake, and that the dangerous-looking man was watching with steely eyes even more interested than hers.

"Tell me, Constable Baker," Gareth asked. "What is your word of honor worth?"

CONSTABLE

GARETH THE VANIR looked up as the door to the hospital room opened, admitting Eveth Baker and Jackeith Grodray. He saw another pair of armed Constables guarding the room from the outside before the door closed again firmly.

Talyarkinash had been seated next to Gareth's hospital bed, where she had been eagerly consuming some medical article on her pocketcomm. She put it down now and looked up expectantly.

Gareth considered the several empty dishes on the tray stretched across the bed. He hadn't felt the need to be in a private clinic, but had been unable to convince anyone else that he felt fine.

At least they had been feeding him better food than he remembered from his previous hospital stay, and enough for three people. And he had been able to transform himself back into a human, well, a Vanir, although that had left him so exhausted that he had been at the mercy of the two cops. But they had only brought him here.

On each trip to the tiny restroom in the last three days,

Gareth had measured his new, Vanir body against the door frame, until he had finally stopped growing.

Seven feet, four inches. Three hundred and forty pounds, but he would need to get back to the gym and PT soon. It had been almost two weeks since his last morning run around the gym level, back at The Arsenal. He hadn't shaved in a week, and his hair was far too long for Sky Patrol regulations.

Eveth Baker was closer, with Grodray standing off to one side and a full stride behind her. Something about the man left Gareth concerned. The eyes were too bright, too knowing for a simple police detective.

"Some of them got away," Baker began without preamble. "Maximus, Maiair, Yooyar, and Zorge being the most important to elude capture. We've caught many others. Your two helpers, Morty and Xiomber, have also vanished. For now."

"For now," Gareth agreed. "I only promised Maximus a one day head start, so he's already gotten more than I bargained for."

"You think you'll be chasing after him, Dankworth?" she challenged.

"I am a Field Agent of the Earth Force Sky Patrol, Constable Baker," he responded solemnly. "A cop, among other things. So yes, I'll be going after him as soon as you let me out of this hospital bed."

"How?" she asked.

"I can't go back to Earth. Ever. That much is certain," Gareth said. "I had to sacrifice everything, with Talyarkinash's help, to do something crazy enough to defeat that man, however temporarily he escaped me afterwards. He becomes my next mission."

"You're not a cop here, Dankworth," she noted angrily.

"You are an illegally-enhanced, alien creature whose very existence is a crime."

"Yes," he agreed. "That still doesn't change my task."

"And if we won't allow it?"

"You let me know when you have someone who can stop Marc Sarzynski, Constable," Gareth retorted. "Because nothing I've seen, read, or heard in the *Accord of Souls* suggests the sort of ruthlessness to fight that man nose to nose."

"I could," she suggested.

Gareth studied the woman for a second. Six foot seven. Built like an East German Olympic swimmer, with a long, feminine frame covered over with muscles.

And a brain like a computer.

"You might," Gareth made a peace offering. "But I know how that man thinks. He was my best friend for many years before he turned to evil and lost himself. And you are at the top of what a geneticist like Talyarkinash here could do to improve you. Marc's not. Especially now that he knows what lengths I was willing to go to in order to stop him."

"You're it, then?" Eveth sneered.

Gareth shrugged, and addressed his next words as much to the Nari scientist next to his bed, who had become his friend, as the cop looming over him now.

"If I could deliver you his head on a platter today, I would happily walk into a cell for the rest of my life tomorrow," Gareth said. "Or ask you how to erase enough knowledge from my brain that you could shrink me back down and send me home. Until then, I might be the only thing standing between you and the darkness."

He expected Baker to say something more, but her partner placed a silent hand on her shoulder.

Baker nodded and stepped to one side silently.

The Vanir man, Senior Constable Jackeith Grodray stepped up now, into her place.

"You don't know our ways, Gareth," he explained in a calm, deep voice.

Gareth shrugged again, rather than answer. That much was a given. He had been here for all of a week.

"Back home, you were a Field Agent of Sky Patrol, correct?" he asked.

"Correct," Gareth nodded. "Only about a month ago, I got my third ring, and was all set to propose to the woman I loved, the night this all happened."

Grodray nodded in turn, his face turning pensive and serious. He turned to the fourth person in the room.

"Dr. Liamssen," Grodray began in a heavy voice. "You belong in the cell next to Gareth, and normally I would be happy to put you there."

Talyarkinash surprised both of them by standing slowly. She couldn't look the giant man in the eyes, but that was a physical thing, not a measure of her stature. Gareth felt a surge of pride in the woman.

"And?" she asked in a hard, unforgiving voice.

From the look on Grodray's face, she might have gotten the same response, the same look on his face, had she just slapped him. Baker shared Gareth's grin from behind the scene.

"Under the auspices of the Official Secrets Act, I can deputize you into a posse for purposes of supporting efforts of the Constabulary to fight crime, in extreme circumstances."

Gareth had spent enough time around the Nari woman to measure her own shock at those words, ears flat backwards, pupils slitted all the way open, jaw hanging, fur on her neck and arms standing up.

Something niggled at the back of Gareth's mind. He had spent the last three days eating, sleeping, and reading.

"I'm sorry," he said in a concerned voice. "But I don't believe that a Senior Constable has that authority. I don't have the book in front of me to quote the statute, but I have been studying your manual."

Grodray's eyes got big. So did Baker's.

After a moment, the man nodded once and reached into his back pocket. He pulled out his wallet. The badge inside was the standard blue ring of The Constabulary, but then the man opened what looked like a secret compartment to reveal a second badge, smaller and made of platinum.

Eveth Baker gasped.

"You would be correct, Gareth," Grodray conceded carefully. "However, Senior Constable is a cover. I am actually a Prime Investigator with the Constabulary, something roughly equivalent to a Senior Special Agent with Sky Patrol. And that kind of person does have the necessary authority."

Gareth nodded, his own jaw almost on the floor next to Eveth Baker's.

"And under the Official Secrets Act, any disclosure of that information will result in a jail sentence of not less than ten years, so you have been warned."

"How can I help?" Gareth asked. Then he turned to Talyarkinash to include her in the conversation. "How can *we* help?"

"My superiors have come to the same conclusions you have, Field Agent Dankworth," Prime Investigator Grodray intoned seriously. "Your help will be necessary to stop Maximus and his gang, and to return some level of honest government to the systems of the *Accord of Souls*, where too many of them have become infected with corruption. We're not sure how we'll use you, yet, but you represent an entirely new option in our fight against crime."

Gareth nodded.

The underworld had an overlord who had once been one of the most dangerous criminals in the Solar System in Marc Sarzynski.

The Constabulary would need a Star Dragon.

READ MORE!

Be sure to read all of the Star Dragon books!

Birth of the Star Dragon
Flight of the Star Dragon
Call of the Star Dragon
Shadow of the Star Dragon
Trial of the Star Dragon

ABOUT THE AUTHOR

Blaze Ward writes science fiction in the Alexandria Station universe (Jessica Keller, The Science Officer, The Story Road, etc.) as well as several other science fiction universes, such as Star Dragon, the Collective, and more. He also writes odd bits of high fantasy with swords and orcs. In addition, he is the Editor and Publisher of *Boundary Shock Quarterly Magazine*. You can find out more at his website www.blazeward.com, as well as Facebook, Goodreads, and other places.

Blaze's works are available as ebooks, paper, and audio, and can be found at a variety of online vendors. His newsletter comes out monthly, and you can also follow his blog on his website. He really enjoys interacting with fans, and looks forward to any and all questions—even ones about his books!

Never miss a release!
If you'd like to be notified of new releases, sign up for my newsletter.

I will never spam you or use your email for nefarious purposes. You can also unsubscribe at any time.

http://www.blazeward.com/newsletter/

Connect with Blaze!

Web: www.blazeward.com
Boundary Shock Quarterly (BSQ):
https://www.boundaryshockquarterly.com/

facebook.com/KRPBlaze

goodreads.com/Blaze_Ward

ABOUT KNOTTED ROAD PRESS

Knotted Road Press fiction specializes in dynamic writing set in mysterious, exotic locations.

Knotted Road Press non-fiction publishes autobiographies, business books, cookbooks, and how-to books with unique voices.

Knotted Road Press creates DRM-free ebooks as well as high-quality print books for readers around the world.

With authors in a variety of genres including literary, poetry, mystery, fantasy, and science fiction, Knotted Road Press has something for everyone.

Knotted Road Press
www.KnottedRoadPress.com